CASSIDY

A LT. KATE GAZZARA NOVEL BOOK 7

BLAIR HOWARD

CASSIDY

A Lt. Kate Gazzara Novel Book 7
By
Blair Howard

Created with Vellum

DEDICATION

For Jo
As Always

CASSIDY

PROLOGUE

Hank Reese had no idea what was waiting for him just a couple of miles down the road. If he had, he would probably have turned around and taken the longer Frog Lane route home that evening. Evening? Well, it was almost six-thirty so, yes, early evening.

It was already dark; he'd had a couple of beers... Okay, so he'd had four, but being the drinker he was, they'd had no effect on his ability to keep the little machine he was driving on the straight and narrow... the road, that is.

He'd spent most of the afternoon with his buddy Joe, lazing around, watching TV, and just generally hanging out and shooting the shit. They were both in their twenties, no girlfriends—ha, with his schedule how would that even be possible? Now he was on his way home to bed.

His family owned a small dairy farm, and he had to be up at four-thirty in the morning with the cows, literally. They had to be milked and, though he would never admit it to anyone, especially Joe, milking time was his favorite part of the day. It was quiet, the cows were always happy to see him, and dang if they weren't easy to talk to. Not like talking to a girl. Somehow, he always managed to say the wrong thing no matter how hard he tried. *Now cows... Well, they understand, don't they? And they never talk back.*

He made the left turn off Calumet onto Route 18 and cranked up the gas, pushing the little machine to a hair-raising forty-two miles an hour, which would have been exhilarating in daylight. In the dark, however, on the narrow rural road, it was pretty damn dangerous. Dangerous or not, his bed was calling and there was little traffic so on he went, the wind in his face, a knight riding into battle... *Shit!*

He hit the brake, braced himself, closed his eyes, and waited for the impact. It never came. He opened his eyes to find himself on the wrong side of the road, almost nose to nose with a car. The dark vehicle he'd almost smashed into was parked half on and half off the side of the road. *Stupid son of a... What the hell?*

He backed up a little, climbed off the machine, set it on its stand, pulled a flashlight out of the toolbox, took a step forward, and stopped. He took a deep breath then shone the flashlight on the car.

The passenger side of the car's windshield was shattered...

He stepped to the driver's side door and peeked in, the small beam from his flashlight illuminating the inside. The driver's seat was empty, but the passenger side... He gasped. There was a man with a gaping hole where his nose should have been. The dash, console, and window were awash in blood and... "Holy shit!" he whispered, as he staggered two steps backward, fumbling in his pants pocket for his phone.

He dragged it out and punched in 911: nothing. He looked at the screen... *Shit, no service!*

He ran to his bike, hopped on, turned around and drove back the way he'd come, holding his phone in front of his face, waiting for service. Two miles on he was able to make the call and was told by the dispatcher to return to the scene and wait for assistance, and under no circumstances was he to touch anything.

Ten minutes later, and stone-cold sober, he was sitting in the darkness on the shoulder some twenty yards from the car, his elbows on his knees, his head in his hands, wondering what the hell he'd gotten himself into, wishing to hell that instead of being nosey he'd just driven right on by. But deep down he knew that would have been the wrong thing to do. *Unneighborly even.*

He lifted his head quickly; something rustled in the cornfield behind him. With his heart pounding, he sprang to his feet and headed to his bike to retrieve the flashlight.

And then Hank heard the distant wail of approaching sirens.

1

I knew my workday was going to be rough when I woke to find the sun had already set—yes, I was on the night shift—and I'd just showered and was drying my hair when I noticed several gray hairs just above my left temple. *Holy cow... really?*

For a minute I just stood there and stared at them. There are some women I know who would freak out at such a devastating discovery, don a baseball cap, dash to the nearest drug store and grab a box full of chemicals. And I have to tell you that, for a moment I was tempted to do just that, but I didn't. For one thing, I knew no one would notice since I'm a blonde... well, a dark blonde, and second, I was working nights, and only the freaks come out at night, right?

I'd been working the late shift—seven to seven—for the past several months. It came with my promotion to Captain.

Captain Catherine Gazzara. You have to admit, it does have a nice ring to it; the pay's not bad either. But with the promotion came new responsibilities, so it really was no surprise to see those gray hairs. I guess the surprise was that there weren't more of them. I was, after all, forty-two years old. Do I sound like I was obsessing? Maybe I was, but not for long; I had a job to get to.

So, I shrugged, accepted the inevitable, finished my morning routine, drank a cup of lukewarm black coffee, and then dressed in jeans, a white top, and a black leather biker jacket that had set me back a week's pay. I tied my hair back in a ponytail, drank another cup of coffee, and headed out into the burgeoning night.

It was almost seven when I arrived at the police department that Tuesday evening in December, to find my partner, Sergeant Janet Toliver, nervously awaiting me, which was not a good thing and I felt my skin begin to prickle.

"Good evening, Captain," Janet said, unusually formal and looking even more like a teenager than she normally did. Her looks, though, were deceiving. She was a bubbly little thing, only twenty-five years old with red hair, green eyes, an upturned nose, freckles and, well, you get the idea. As I said, looks can be deceiving. The girl was more than capable of handling herself on the job, on the street, and in a scrap. She'd been with me almost two years and had had my back more times than I cared to admit.

"What's up, Janet?" I asked.

"Chief Johnston's waiting for you, in your office." She looked over her shoulder then back at me. "He's been in there for about fifteen minutes. He looks like he's loaded for bear."

"He always looks like that," I said with more confidence than I felt. "What's he doing?"

"Just sitting there with his eyes closed, waiting for you. Was I supposed to ask him what he wanted?"

"No," I replied, pursing my lips.

The Chief waiting in your office can never be a good thing.

I tried to think back on all the cases I'd worked over the last few months and who I might have upset during the course thereof. A cop's life isn't easy these days—not that it ever was. Thirty-eight officers killed nationwide in the line of duty already that year; thank God it was almost over. And God only knew how many false accusations had been leveled at hard-working officers. There was always a perp claiming a cop had roughed them up or someone had forgotten to read them their rights. It had happened to me more than once. But try as I might, I couldn't think of anything I'd done that could have gotten me into trouble, but that didn't mean there wasn't something, something I'd overlooked that had caused a major-league logjam for someone. In this case, the Chief of Police, Wesley Johnston.

And suddenly I felt like I was back in high school, called to the principal's office. Hell, I knew I wasn't the best student in class, so what I could have done wrong was anyone's guess.

"Okay," I said. "I'll go see what he wants. I'll give you a call when we're done."

I adjusted my purse over my shoulder, checked my Glock and badge on my waist, made sure my top was tucked properly into my jeans, and headed to my office. My new office. Another perk of my promotion. I had tons more shelf space, my desk was bigger, there was a round table for meetings with a half-dozen straight-backed chairs, a coffee table and... Lordy, Lordy, a small but comfy couch; I even had a small, personal coffee maker, but that was between me and nobody else.

"Hey, Cap. The Chief is waiting in your office," Lennie Miller shouted from his cubicle as I crossed the situation room. Lennie is a junior detective and something of a computer wiz, another perk of my promotion. I nodded and hurried before he could yell something else.

Chief Johnston was seated on my couch. His long legs stretched out in front and crossed at the ankles, his arms folded across his chest. Had I not known better, I might have thought he was taking a nap.

"Evening, Chief," I said, brightly, closing the door behind me and dumping my bag on my desk. "What's the haps?"

"Catherine. I need to talk to you."

Catherine? He was the only one that ever called me that, and then only when I was in trouble or he wanted to make a serious point. I figured I was in trouble.

"Look," I said, "I can vouch for my team. Whatever the accusations are they are false. Internal Affairs can come talk to me." I blurted the words out before I even realized I was speaking.

"Relax, Kate. You're becoming paranoid. No one has made any accusations..." He paused, like he'd had a sudden thought. "At least that I know of. But the fact that you're so willing to talk to Internal Affairs makes me very nervous."

He wasn't smiling, just stared up at me as if he was waiting for a confession.

"Oh," I said, offhandedly, "you know the old saying: hope for the best but expect the worst." I smiled and slipped behind my desk, shoved the small stack of files aside, folded my hands, and leaned forward.

Even seated as he was, Chief Wesley Johnston cut an imposing figure. He was, as always, impeccably dressed, his uniform pressed to perfection, which was probably why he was stretched out the way he was.

"Kate, fifteen minutes ago a call came in, a report of a robbery-homicide on Rural Route 18 just before it intersects with Pellmont Road. The car's registered to a Jack Logan, an accountant. I want you and your team to handle it."

He unfolded his arms, sat up straight, rubbed his shiny bald head, and looked at me across the desk, obviously waiting for me to speak.

"Sure, Chief, but... isn't that area kind of iffy for jurisdiction? I'm not going to run into an angry Sheriff White, am I?"

"It's within the city limits, but not by much... maybe ten or twenty yards. You shouldn't have any problems. I'll talk to Whitey. But, Kate, I need for you to be extra careful with this one." The Chief swallowed hard, as if he had a sore throat.

"Of course. Can I ask why?"

"I knew the man. Well, I did, but not as well as my neighbor did."

He cleared his throat and continued, "My neighbor, Jimmy, and I became friends the day he and his wife and kids moved in about twelve years ago. Our kids played together. Our wives went shopping together. Holidays and birthdays, we always spent at least some time together."

Chief Johnston had a smile on his face, something I

rarely saw. Then the smile disappeared and he said, "That's how I became acquainted with the victim, through Jimmy Boyd. Jack Logan was Jimmy's sister's ex-husband. Logan's ex-wife's name is Cynthia, by the way."

"I see," I said.

"According to Jimmy, they preferred Jack's company to Cynthia's, even though she was Jimmy's own sister. I met Jack and Cynthia on more than one occasion at Jimmy's house, and quite frankly, I could see why. Cynthia was a... Well, never mind."

The Chief cleared his throat again. "Jack was just a nice guy. A good conversationalist, knowledgeable, knew a little something about everything, but he wasn't a know-it-all. He was a good guy. You felt comfortable around him. It's a real shame."

"And what about Cynthia, the victim's ex-wife? You were about to say something and then stopped... So what's she like?" I asked.

"She's a trip..." The Chief shook his head. "Has a foul mouth. Laughs at her own jokes though they were never that funny. I think she's in denial about her age, wants to be twenty-one again but that ship sailed about twenty years ago."

"Is she a suspect?" I asked.

He thought for a minute, then said, "She could be. According to Jimmy, Cynthia wasn't happy that Jack remarried. Be careful when you talk to her, Kate. She's an alligator looking for someone to eat. Don't let it be you."

He shook his head, ran a hand over its shiny surface, did that slicky thing men do with their mustaches, then stood and smoothed the front of his pants.

"Oh, and Catherine, if there *is* anything Internal Affairs might be wanting to talk to me about, I want to know about it. I don't want to be blindsided, so tell me... Now!"

"There's nothing, Chief. Not a thing!"

He nodded, turned and walked out of the room, closing the door behind him.

I let out a long sigh of relief, looked at the stack of files on my desk and sighed again. I'm no desk jockey; never will be. It was something I'd made clear when Chief Johnston offered me my promotion to captain. I'm a detective, not an administrator. Paperwork gives me gray hairs, literally, as I'd found out just that morning.

So I slid the stack of files back to the center of my desk, patted the one on top gently and smiled to myself, feeling proud that if nothing else I had at least touched them. Then I grabbed my purse, called Janet and, like Captain Jack Sparrow, headed out to the edge of my world, the Chattanooga city limits and the end of my jurisdiction, stopping only to fill my thirty-two-ounce flask at the incident room urn. Yuk!

2

Driving along Pellmont Road, even in daylight, was like heading off into a David Lynch movie. At night, it was a dark, lonely narrow two-lane at the northwest city limit dotted here and there by glowing porch lights set back off the road like unblinking eyes. Occasionally, we'd see the gleaming green and gold eyes of a raccoon or possum caught in the headlights, sometimes in the middle of the road, sometimes in the tall grass on the roadside.

Finally, in the distance, we saw the cluster of red and blue flashing lights of the police vehicles and the red and white lights of an ambulance and, every few seconds a bright flash of white light. Mike Willis' CSI team had positioned three portable high-intensity lights and were already working the scene and taking pictures.

"If they're taking pictures, that means Doc is already here," I said.

Doctor Richard Sheddon, Hamilton County's Chief Medical Examiner, was one of the few people I could rely on to keep me sane in a world where death is the norm rather than the exception. He was, still is, my friend, a rock to lean on when things get tough. He's not a big man... well, not tall anyway. He's around five-eight, in his late fifties, overweight, almost totally bald, with a round face that usually sports half-glasses and a jovial expression. He treats unnatural death as if it's nothing more than part of the natural order of things, which I suppose it is.

"He makes me nervous," Janet said.

"Doc? Why?" I asked, glancing sideways at her.

"I don't know," she said, keeping her eyes on the road as she negotiated a sharp bend. "He doesn't really talk, does he? He barks. And whenever I have to meet him at the Forensic Center, he offers me coffee cake with raspberries or cherries or something that resembles something he's just removed from a body." Janet pulled her lips down at the corners. "He's weird."

I smiled. "Yeah, I suppose he is, a little. That's why I like him."

"I'm not talking bad about him. I like him well enough but... well, he makes me nervous. Sorry. I'm just saying."

"No need to be sorry. I understand what you're saying. He's been talking to the dead for more than twenty-five years. So yes, he's different. Don't tell me that wouldn't make you a little weird, too."

She nodded, then shrugged as she pulled up and parked behind one of the cruisers.

"I guess you've got a point," she said, as she snapped on a pair of latex gloves while I grabbed my coffee from the cup holder, and we exited the car.

"Wait," I said, putting a hand on her arm.

"Why? What's wrong?"

"Nothing. I just want to look for a minute."

Mike Willis's crime scene unit was parked almost in the ditch some twenty yards or so back from a metallic silver sedan that appeared to have run off the road almost into the cornfield, and it would have, had its passenger side front wheel not dropped into a shallow ditch.

I stood for a moment, staring at the sedan, then looked back down the road; beyond the dome of light put out by Mike's lights it was dark, really dark.

"Come on," I said as I walked toward the car. There were no skid marks that I could see, so it didn't look like the driver had lost control of the vehicle and swerved off the road. None of the tires were flat. I wondered if the airbags hadn't gone off. It looked more like it had been deliberately parked, that the driver had intentionally parked out in the middle of nowhere.

"Hey, Kate," Doc said from somewhere behind me. "You brought coffee and something to eat, I hope. Hey, Janet. Nice night for it, right?"

"I think there may be a Twinkie from 1998 in my glove box. You can have it if you want," I said, handing him my coffee without looking up as I studied the outside of the car.

I took a pair of latex gloves from my pocket and put them on, then took a step forward... A head bobbed up above the car's roof on the far side of the vehicle, the passenger side.

"Hold on, Kate. Give me a second. I'm not quite done here yet."

It was Mike Willis, standing at the edge of the ditch, taking pictures. I nodded.

He disappeared again and a couple of seconds later reappeared.

"Okay," he said. "I'm done. We haven't opened the doors or moved anything... yet. The flatbed truck should be here soon, but take your time."

The car was a Chrysler Sebring and, thanks to the Chief, I already knew that it was registered to a Jack L. Logan. I took another step forward and shined my flashlight in the driver's side window. Logan, what was left of him, was in the passenger seat, slumped against the door, his head lolled to the right resting against the door frame. There was what looked like a bullet wound to his left temple, and his left eye and most of his nose were missing. There was a hole in the windshield surrounded by blood spatter and a large smear of thick, viscous blood on the dash...

Geez, he must have been shot in the back of the head, thrown forward and then... And then what? The killer pulled him upright, positioned him? Why is he in the passenger seat? What the hell? How the hell? Why?

I heard a car door open nearby and then a moment later slam shut again, then the rustle of plastic wrap. I stood, turned, and stepped aside so that Janet could take a look.

"I had to run out of my house," Doc said as he stuffed the wrapper in his pocket with one hand and took a bite of the Twinkie in the other. "No time to eat anything. Umm, I haven't had one of these in a coon's age." He smacked his lips.

"Where's my coffee, Doc?"

"Oh... yes, sorry." He returned to my car, retrieved the cup from the hood.

"Here you go," he said, after taking a huge gulp and then handing it to me.

I hefted the cup; it felt like it was almost empty. I cut him a dirty look. He grinned back at me unperturbed.

"What do you think, Doc?" I asked.

"Pretty damn good for 1998..." he mumbled, his mouth full. "Oh, you mean... Well, probably a nine-millimeter weapon, judging by the exit wound. Anything larger would have removed most of his face, not to mention the windshield. He was also shot in the left temple. There's another exit wound at the right side of his head."

He finished the Twinkie, licked his fingers, dried them on his pants, snapped on a pair of purple latex gloves, then held out his hand for my coffee. I handed it to him and he closed his eyes and took a huge gulp.

"Oh my," I said sarcastically. "Would you like some coffee?" I looked from him to the cup and back again.

"Took you long enough to ask," he grumbled, then took another sip and handed it back to me... empty. *Damn it, Doc!*

I hefted the cup, sighed resignedly, handed it off to Janet, opened the driver's side door, leaned inside for a closer look at the body, and said, "So, time of death?" The inside of the car had that coppery smell about it. *Geez, I hate the smell of blood.*

"You know better than to ask that question when we have yet to extract the body from the vehicle... Judging from how much the blood has coagulated... not long, two hours, three at the most. Once we get him out of there, I'll check the liver temperature... My question is, though: what the hell is he doing in the passenger seat?"

It was a question I was asking myself, so I didn't bother to answer.

"So," I said, checking my watch—it was just after eight, "it was called in at six-thirty-one, so that narrows it down to... sometime between five and six-thirty... Hey, there's something under the seat." I reached beneath the seat and felt a soft, thick object. It was a wallet. I opened it.

"Jack L. Logan," I muttered. "I knew that."

There was a wedding picture of him and his wife, several credit cards in designated slots, but no cash. *Robbery, then? Petty cash? Not something to kill for, but I've seen people shot dead for the price of a burger, so...* I let the thought go, extricated myself from the car, and stood back, the wallet still in my hands. I wouldn't know if anything was missing until I spoke with his wife... *his current wife.*

"Janet?" I called.

"Yeah," she replied. She was standing on the road with Mike Willis.

"Any word on the tow truck?" I asked.

"On their way," Willis replied. "They called and said they're about five minutes out."

I nodded, stared at the wallet, then at the interior of the car, and shook my head. *I just don't get it... If he was jacked... surely the jacker would have been in the passenger seat. And where the hell did he go? At five-thirty it would have been getting dark. It's more than three miles back to civilization. Did someone pick him up? Did anyone see him? I kinda doubt it. Why here?*

This was not a strategic execution. This was a murder either for the joy of killing or for the money. I was leaning toward the second option. Jack Logan was in the wrong place at the wrong time. A carjacking that escalated. Maybe. Maybe he picked up a hitchhiker.

No good deed goes unpunished... but again, why was he in the passenger seat?

I snapped a couple photos of the body with my iPhone: a close-up of the head and the wound to the temple. Then I went around to the passenger side of the car, opened the rear door and snapped a couple of pics of the wound to the back of his head. *How the hell did the killer do that... and why? Two... of them?*

"Where's the person who phoned this in?" I asked Doc, closing the car door.

Doc shrugged; he was focused on the paramedics who were beginning to extricate the body.

I looked around. There was a weird glow over the scene from the LED lights: shadows, flickering shadows as the techs went about their tasks. Darker shadows beyond the reach of the lights. Beyond that, nothing but blackness.

I saw three uniformed officers standing together beside one of the cruisers. There was a man with them. He was talking to one of the officers. *That's him,* I thought, *has to be.*

He was wearing jeans, a flannel shirt and a heavy jacket, shifting from one foot to the other, back and forth. I walked over and joined the group.

"Detective Gazzara, this is Hank Reese," the uniformed officer said. "He called it in."

"Thank you, Officer," I said.

The officer nodded, stepped backward and away to join the other three who were now helping Doc and Janet with the body.

"Hello, Mr. Reese," I said. "Thank you for staying. I

really appreciate it. What can you tell me? Oh, just give me a minute, please. I'll be right back."

Out of the corner of my eye, I'd spotted the flatbed arriving. I stepped over to the truck where Mike Willis was talking to the driver.

"Mike. Don't let them take it away until I've had a word. I'm talking to that guy over there. I should be finished with him shortly, okay?"

"You got it, Captain," Willis replied.

I went back to my car and retrieved my iPad.

Hank Reese was a thin guy with a long neck in his late twenties. He had that farmer's build: wiry but muscular from bailing hay or whatever it is those people do all day.

"Now, Mr. Reese," I said, turning on the recording app. "I'm going to record our conversation, please tell me that you consent."

He did. I asked him to provide his name, address and phone number for the record. I added the time and place, and then said, "Talk to me, Mr. Reese."

"Well, see, it was like this. I was coming home from my buddy Joe's house... that's down along Calumet off 18, you know, where the Gas City is on the corner."

I nodded as he pointed off into the distance. Then I looked around for the beat-up truck I imagined he likely drove, but I didn't see one.

"So you were walking, then?"

He looked at me like I was crazy.

"What? Walking? Course not. I was ridin' that." He turned and pointed to a spot between two cruisers.

I looked at it, then at him, then at it again, and then I

couldn't help but smile. It was a bright blue, Alibaba electric motorcycle.

"That's yours?" I asked, smiling.

"Yeah, so?"

I just shook my head, then said, "Go on, Mr. Reese."

"Well. As I said, I was comin' back from Joe's. We'd just been hanging out, had a few beers, watched a couple movies, just shootin' the shit. Oh, pardon me, ma'am." Reese paused, looked embarrassed.

I said nothing.

"So I was heading back. See, I gotta be at the milkin' shed by four-thirty each morning. They get ornery if I'm late... the cows, you know?" I nodded and he continued, "Anyway, I didn't see it, see. An' I almost run into it. The car, right there; it was just parked... At first, I thought maybe the dude had been drinking and drove into the ditch. But then when I got closer, I could see he hadn't... drove into the ditch, at least I didn't think so. It looked like he'd tried to park but drove a little too far off the pavement." He paused again, his mind obviously somewhere else.

"See, I lost my father last year. He'd gone to start one of our tractors and had a heart attack right there in the seat."

"I'm sorry," I said, wondering where the hell he was going with it.

"Thank you," he said. "But I thought maybe, that is, maybe this man had the same thing happen to him, a heart attack, like. I got a flashlight in the toolbox." He nodded toward the bike. "You never know when it's going to run out of juice... So I shined it in the car. But when I got close to it, I saw all the blood." He shook his head and ran his hand through his hair again. "I just about lost my lunch... know what I mean?"

I nodded, then said, "Did you touch anything, Mr. Reese?"

"No, ma'am. I freaked out. I went back to my bike and called y'all. Part of me wanted to ride away and get home, but I figured that wouldn't look all that good. Besides, I wouldn't want to be just left out here if it was me. Even if I was dead. I'd hope someone would wait around to make sure I got found."

I gathered a few more details from him and informed him that I'd be checking his alibi.

"Of course, Detective. I'm telling the truth. No doubt about that," he stuttered.

"Mr. Reese, did you notice anything unusual when you pulled up, or while you were waiting? Another set of tail-lights? Did anyone pass you going in the opposite direction? Did you hear anything strange when you stopped? Did you smell anything unusual?"

"I held my breath when I saw that body in there." He looked at the ground and I could tell he was giving it his best shot to remember everything. "I'm sorry. There wasn't anything."

"Thank you, Mr. Reese," I said. "I'll need a formal statement from you. You can do it here, or at the department later tonight; your choice."

He nodded. "I need to get to work. Can we do it later, say after three this afternoon?"

I told him he could, gave him my business card, and told him someone would be expecting him. He looked at it and then at me. "I never met a female detective before." He looked at me and grinned.

"All the ones you met were men, huh?" I said as I started to walk away.

"Oh, no. I never... I mean... I never met even one detective before."

He was trying to clarify even though I knew what he meant. I just liked to put people on the spot. It was my job and hard to stop when I found it so much fun.

I watched him climb onto the incongruously tiny electric bike and ride wobbly away, then I walked to where Jack Logan's car was being winched up onto the back of the flatbed.

Doc Sheddon was at the back of the ambulance with his patient, Jack Logan. The body was in a bag ready for transportation to Doc's little shop of horrors.

3

———

"Okay. Guess what happened while you were interviewing the witness?" Janet said as we drove back toward the city. She waited two seconds and then said, "I'll tell you because you'll never guess. We were loading the victim onto the gurney, and his cell phone fell out of his pocket."

"That's a plus," I said. "Anything interesting on it?"

"Dunno. It's got a passcode, so I'll get Miller on it as soon as we get back to the office. The uniforms are going to inform the victim's wife, but we need to talk to her, too, so I thought I'd take Ann with me... You'll be going to Doc's place, right?"

I nodded.

"You know," she said, "two women: his wife and his ex-wife... maybe he was having an affair? If there were any domestic issues... well, you never know, do you? We could have it wrapped up by morning."

"That's what you think, is it, that he was having an affair?" I asked.

"I don't know what to think," she replied. "He seems like a good guy to me, based on what the Chief told you, but... Look, I ran his record before we left the PD. He has no priors. Not so much as a traffic ticket. You said there was no cash in his wallet, but his credit cards were all still there. Maybe someone was trying to make it look like a robbery."

"We don't know that all of his cards were there," I said. "Not yet, anyway. Yes, take Ann and go talk to the wife. See what you can find out."

Detective Ann Robar was a transfer from another department. I'd known her a long time. At forty-four, she was a couple of years older than me and had more than twenty years as a cop, fifteen of them as a detective. Although Janet's perkiness got on her nerves sometimes, Ann had been showing rookie Janet the ropes. Which I appreciated.

"I want Hawk to stick with Mike Willis," I said. "I want that car processed ASAP."

"I'll call him," Janet said.

It was almost ten o'clock when we arrived back at the PD that evening. The weather was good, though cold, and I began to wish I'd brought a heavier coat.

Janet dropped off Logan's phone with Miller, then she and Ann left to go talk to Sheila Logan while I went to my office with a stop along the way, in the incident room for a refill of my coffee mug. I could have made my own, but I just couldn't be bothered.

I checked my messages—fortunately there were none—and then spent the next hour going through the recording of the Hank Reese interview, making notes, and listing questions that still needed to be answered. I had it at the back of my mind that I was dealing with something more than a carjacking gone wrong. Those two head wounds bothered me.

I took out my phone, pulled up the images I'd shot inside Logan's car, and sent them to my printer. Then I taped them up on the whiteboard and, with a black marker, drew a large question mark alongside the photos of the head wounds.

I started the list of questions:

1. Why shoot him twice?
2. Why was Logan in the passenger seat?
3. Why take the cash but leave the wallet and the credit cards behind?
4. One perp or two?

I had no answers, nor would I until I'd talked to Doc and Mike Willis.

I leaned back in my chair, put my hands behind my head, and closed my eyes, trying to imagine how it could have happened. I couldn't. All I could see were two dark, unidentifiable images of someone in the driver's seat and someone in the back seat.

Two people? Hitchhikers? I doubt it. No one in their right mind would risk picking up two strangers, not these days. Friends, then? Possibly. Shit! Who the hell knows?

I let myself fall forward onto my feet, grabbed my coffee and, with a final look at the images on the board, I left and headed over to the medical examiner's office.

4

W hen I pulled into the parking lot out front of Doc Sheddon's Forensic Center, it was empty, no vehicles; it was, after all, almost midnight so I had to assume that the front door was locked. That being so, I drove around back. The parking lot there was also empty, except for Doc's car. I parked next to it and sat for a moment, as I always did before entering what I liked to think of as the dead zone, gathering myself for the ordeal that was to come.

The Forensic Center—I often wondered why they called it that, because the only forensics that went on inside were medical examinations; Mike Willis ran CSI from a suite of offices and a lab inside the PD. Anyway, the Forensic Center was a small, unremarkable building located on Amnicola just three blocks from the police department— The Police Services Center. Try saying that three times quickly when you've had a couple of glasses of red.

Doc's place was, and still is, comprised of a suite of three offices, two examination rooms, several labs and a nasty little section—I don't know what else to call it—where Carol Oats, the resident forensic anthropologist, stripped unidentified, unclaimed bodies down to their bare bones, literally. I hate the Forensic Center.

I hit the buzzer at the outer door and Doc's tinny voice asked, "That you, Kate?"

I confirmed that it was indeed me, the lock clicked, and I pushed the door open and stepped inside.

I made my way along the corridor to the first of the two autopsy rooms and found Doc inside bending over a naked body on one of the three stainless steel autopsy tables.

He, Doc, was dressed from head to toe in green scrubs, a face shield, and a vast rubber apron already liberally smeared with blood. He'd already made the "Y" incision and peeled back the flesh revealing the ribcage still in situ; he looked like frickin' Frankenstein.

"Better cover up," he called as I stood in the doorway. "And hurry up, you're letting all the cold air out."

I took a deep breath, sighed, turned, and did as he asked. I joined him a couple of minutes later dressed in a pale blue Tyvek coverall, safety glasses, and a breathing mask.

The naked body on the table was, of course, that of Jack Logan. His clothes had been bagged and tagged and set aside ready for transportation to Mike Willis' department for processing.

"Don't tell me you dragged Carol in at this time of night," I said, eyeing the evidence bags.

"I did. You just missed her."

I approached the table and stood opposite him, Logan's body between us.

"So, Doc," I said resignedly. "Tell me what we've got."

"White male, one hundred-ninety-three pounds, five feet ten and one-half inches tall, dead as the proverbial dodo bird. Cause of death... one of two gunshot wounds to the head. It's impossible to tell which shot killed him, because it's impossible to determine which was fired first. Either one would have killed him, instantly. My considered opinion is that... he was shot first from the driver's seat, in the left temple, then in the back of the head, probably by someone sitting in the back seat, though why... Well, one can only speculate; it was certainly overkill."

"So," I said, "it could have been a carjacking?"

"It could indeed, which would account for him being in the passenger seat. But carjackers usually want only the car, don't they? They usually toss the driver... So why would they take the vehicle and its owner, and add kidnapping and, in this case, murder to their crime? No, I'm not sold on carjacking."

"What about an old-fashioned robbery?" I asked.

"Nope. You see, he was shot in the side of the head, but that might have been an accident. Whoever was driving was probably pointing the gun at him, may not have had any intention of actually killing him. But say as they are driving, the car hits a pothole or the shoulder, and the gun goes off... but that still doesn't explain the bullet to the back of the head."

"Execution style, you think?" It made sense, but then again, it didn't.

"Your guess is as good as mine," Doc said with a shrug.

"Anything else?" I asked, somewhat dejected.

"I'll be able to tell you what he ate for dinner in an hour

or so. Might be helpful for tracking his movements." Doc handed the file to me to look over. "The weapons were both probably nine-millimeter. Both bullets exited so I won't find them, maybe a fragment or two, but that's all."

"That narrows it down to just three-fourths of a haystack to find that needle," I replied. "Time of death?"

He shrugged. "It was nine-oh-four when I checked the liver temp. It was ninety-five point two. Normal body temperature is ninety-eight point six. The body normally cools at a rate of one point five degrees per hour, so between five-thirty and six-thirty, give or take a few minutes either way."

I looked at the diagram that showed where the bullets entered and exited the victim's head. "All right, Doc. I'll let you finish up here. Call me if you find anything new. When can I have the report?" I handed the slim file back to him.

"When it's done, Kate, when it's done. Now, if you're going... well, you know the way out," Doc said as he grabbed a set of bone shears and positioned himself over Jack Logan's torso. He was about to remove the ribcage, and I wasn't about to hang around to watch. I hated that part; the crunch and crack of bones. I had to get out of there.

"Thanks, Doc. Not going to wish me 'good luck'? No 'let's be careful out there'? Nothing?"

"Don't forget to lock the door when you leave," Doc said without looking up. "And let's be careful out there."

I smiled, did as I was told, left through the rear door, and walked to my car, my mind already churning with possibilities. As I punched the starter button and drove slowly back to the department—it took all of two minutes—I began to think again about the location of the two entry wounds and how the body was positioned in the passenger seat.

Logan had been shot in the left temple. The impact of the bullet would have shoved his body to the right. Then, he was shot in the back of the head at point-blank range. The stippling of gunshot residue around the entry was plain to see. The impact from that wound should have thrown his body forward, but he was sitting upright in the passenger seat.

I sat for a moment in the parking lot at the rear of the PD and pulled up the images I'd taken with my iPhone: *seat belt's not fastened... hmm.*

It wasn't much, but I felt like it was at least a little grease to get the gears moving. I couldn't even say why. So much of police work is guesswork based on a hunch, and I'll even go so far as to say divine intervention. I think maybe it's God's way of helping people like me stay sane when we have to face so much insanity every day. If He didn't drop a clue directly in our laps every now and then... well; my own opinion, of course. Anyway, something about those tiny images triggered a memory and I had to check it out.

So, instead of checking in with my team, I snuck into the elevator and went down to the basement—to the morgue, this one being where the cold case files are stored, not dead bodies.

The morgue is a sad place that few of us visit more than the obligatory once a year—to update the files we've never solved but put to rest, nonetheless. Somehow, though, I always felt comfortable down there among the lost. Not because I was particularly proud that I'd been able to shift a few of them to the closed list, but because I knew I'd made a difference, and would continue to do so. But that was not why I was there that day. As I said, my cell phone images had triggered a memory and... a name.

Some twenty minutes later I found what I was looking for.

"Ah-ha!" I said, breaking the stillness in the room. "There you are, Mr. Cappy T. Mallard."

Who wouldn't remember a name like that? More to the point, who would name their child Cappy? It must have been hell for the kid, having to go through middle and high school with a name like that.

I heaved the cardboard banker's box down from the shelf, carried it to a nearby table, and lifted the lid. The murder book was at the top of the pile of paperwork: reports, interviews, etc., etc. I picked it up, opened it, and flipped quickly through the pages to the photographs, and there he was. It was as if I'd taken the photos myself. Cappy was in the passenger seat of his car. The positioning was almost identical to that of Jack Logan, as was the cause of death: one shot to the temple and one to the back of the head. Cappy's car had been discovered in an industrial park about a mile away from Rural Road 18.

I closed the murder book, put it back in the box, put the lid back on, and then hauled it over to the elevator.

I dumped the box on my desk and returned to the incident room.

Lennie Miller was seated at his desk between two stacks of files, one on either side of his desktop. A third, sloppy but smaller stack of papers was in his inbox; his outbox contained only a couple of single sheets of paper. His laptop was closed and there was an empty coffee cup in front of him.

Lennie was the fourth member of my team. Younger looking than his twenty-eight years and wearing a dark blue, two-piece suit with a white T-shirt. He was tall, maybe five-eleven, with the soft almost pudgy build of a guy into all things techie, but a happy kind of individual with one of those "unshaved look" beards that made him look both scruffy and handsome at the same time. Me? It did nothing for me. He was a good guy, though, and still lived at home to help out his widowed mom.

"What do you have for me, Lennie?" I asked, startling him.

"Oh, hi. I didn't see you come in." He coughed, as he usually did before he started to explain what he was doing. "This was pretty simple." He held up Logan's Samsung phone.

I could see he was about to dive right into a long-winded explanation, so I put my hand up to stop him. I had little interest in what he did to make things work, or his expertise at hacking, computers, phones, codes, GPS, or the Dark Web. My only interest was in the results of what he did.

"I know you're good at what you do, Lennie. Just tell me," I said. "Were you able to unlock it?"

"No problem. He used his wife's birthday for his pass-code. You'd be surprised at how many people do that. I wouldn't recommend it. It's too easy to figure out. Plus, anyone can get access to all your basic personal info, you know, the stuff people say isn't important like birthdays and anniversaries and the kind of cars you've owned. It's really rather spooky how much you can get from—"

Geez, he's Tim Clarke made over. Are they all like that, I wonder?

"Spare me the lecture on internet fraud, Lennie," I said impatiently. "Just tell me what you found?" I gave him a quick smile. He was a chatty Cathy. But he was amazing when it came to the gadgets... Not as good as Tim, but better than I probably deserved.

"It looks like the last person he spoke to was his wife, Sherri, at five-oh-eight," Miller said. "The call originated from somewhere in this area here."

He opened his laptop and turned it to face me. I knew what I was looking at. It was a map of Chattanooga pinpointing all the cell phone towers and where our victim's phone had pinged. There were three towers within the radius we were looking at where Jack had called his wife. I looked at my watch and hoped Janet and Ann would be back soon.

This was good information, which of course prompted more questions. "He must have just gotten off work,

I said. "What businesses are there in and around that area that are open at five o'clock in the afternoon?" I mused.

"Good question. I'll take a look," Miller offered.

"Thanks. And I'll want a full background on him too. I'll be in my office. Let me know what you find out."

5

I t was more than two hours later when I finally heard back from Doc Sheddon.

"Our friend had a burger and a couple of beers just before his demise," Doc said without saying hello. "Onion rings, too. I don't think he was watching his weight."

"Wow. That helps a lot, Doc," I said, sarcastically, and suddenly realizing how hungry I was.

"He had no tattoos, no distinguishing marks. A couple of moles he should have had checked out, but it's too late for that now, of course. He was a plain Jane if ever there was one," Doc said sadly.

"How about trace? Anything?"

"On the body? Nothing I wouldn't expect to find. No foreign hairs, particles... Both bullets exited, as one might expect from a close-quarter wound. No fragments. The shot to the left temple was fired from about twenty-six inches. The one to the back of the head was a contact wound. Other than that, the state of the corpse was quite unre-markable."

"Okay, Doc. Thanks. I'll share it with the team," I said, my mind already starting to piece together some possible directions we could take.

"Yeah, well, don't say I never gave you anything," he grumbled.

"You know I'd never do that, Doc. You're one of my favorite people. And I've only got two."

"There are *two* people who'll tolerate you? Just remember I'm paid to. Who's the other, I wonder?" The smirk in his voice was evident.

"I could tell you but... well, you know how the saying goes," I said. "Would you mind emailing the photos to me, please?"

He said he would and I hung up, just as there was a knock on my door.

"Come in," I called.

"Hi Cap, do you have time for us?" Ann Robar said as she stuck her head inside.

"Sure," I said and set my cold case file aside and picked up what was left of my now cold cup of coffee. "Come on in; sit down; talk to me. What did you learn from Mrs. Logan?"

Ann sat on the couch. Janet took one of the chairs from the table, turned it around to face the middle of the room, and sat down.

Ann Robar was a striking woman, not quite a beauty but... well, striking. Her closely cropped hair, prematurely graying, framed an oval face. Her hazel eyes were clear and intense, though the crow's feet indicated that the woman had spent far too long in the sun without protection, and now her skin was suffering for it. At five-ten, she was almost two inches shorter than me, but she carried herself well... almost arrogantly. She was short on patience and didn't take crap from anyone. She was also married with two teenage boys, both of them still in high school. She was a senior detective and a good one. Could have been a higher rank, but family was her priority, and I admired her dedication to them. She was dressed, as she almost always was, in a white T-shirt and jeans. I don't think I ever saw her wear slacks or a blouse, certainly never in a skirt.

"She already knew her husband was dead," Ann said. "The uniforms had informed her. She seemed genuinely distraught."

She opened her iPad, flipped through several screens, then said, "Mrs. Sherri Logan, age forty-two, was his second wife. They married in 2005, so they were married for almost fourteen years. They had no children. She said that they had their problems, like all couples do, but the good times outweighed the bad. I saw nothing in her behavior that indicated she might have had anything to do with his death." She looked at Janet.

Janet nodded and said, "She said he called her after work and told her he was going to have a beer, something to eat, and maybe watch something on ESPN, and he'd be home by ten. She also said she had a headache and went to bed early, around nine. The next she knew was when the uniforms were knocking on her door."

"We asked her if he stayed out often," Ann said, "and if he was in the habit of coming home late. She said usually only if the Packers or the Braves were playing, but sometimes, whenever he'd had a rough day, he'd stop off somewhere and watch whatever's on, just to relax.

"She also claimed that she isn't into sports and doesn't like to drink, so in deference to her he usually watched the games at a sports bar. He was never out later than eleven and gave her no reason to worry about him, where he was or what he was doing. He treated her well, so she saw nothing wrong with him blowing off a little steam on his own, enjoying what he liked, baseball and football."

"What about enemies?" I asked.

"Sherri couldn't think of anyone who would want to hurt her husband," Janet said. "Apparently, he must have been quite saintly, an all-around good guy. She handled the money. They had a healthy bank account and were saving for a trip to Australia. She said that Jack wanted to go to the place furthest from where they lived but still speak English."

"Nobody's that good," I said. "I've asked Miller to run backgrounds on Logan, his wife, and his ex-wife, so we'll soon know." I paused, then said, "So do we know where he was, which bar?" I asked.

"No," Janet said, "Sherri mentioned several favorites, most of them on his way home from the office, but he'd been at a meeting with a client yesterday on the other side of town. So where he might have stopped off on the way home, she just didn't know."

"Did you get a list?" I asked.

"Yes, of course," Ann said. "D'you want a copy?"

"Not right now, but we need to check them all, no matter where he was last night. We need to find out who his friends were." I stood, went to the board, and with a marker added the words "Bars?" and "Friends?" to the list.

"Well," I said, sitting down again and leaning back in my chair. "Miller's checking the businesses in the area. Until he brings me a list, we wait. In the meantime..." I checked my watch. It was almost four in the morning. "We can't do anything now, not until morning, which it already is..." *Damn, we can't work like this. We need to be working days.*

Thankfully, I had the authority to change our schedule. A handy perk that came with my new rank.

"Go home, both of you. We're switching to the day shift. Tell Lennie to go home too. Get some sleep, a couple of hours anyway, and then go check Logan's place of work. Talk to his co-workers. We'll meet back here at ten o'clock. By then we should know something, okay?"

"Thank God we're back on days," Ann said. "What about Hawk?"

"He's with Mike Willis processing Logan's car," I said. "They should be done in time for breakfast."

They should have been, but they weren't. Anyway, Janet and Ann left my office, leaving me with my thoughts, and I had plenty.

Did Jack Logan have an encounter with a lady of questionable reputation and take her out to Rural Route 18, where things got out of hand? It happens, as I well knew, and with a guy whose entire existence seemed to be as vanilla as his was, I couldn't help but think the worst. It was always the quiet ones that had the dirtiest secrets.

"But Doc would have found proof of that, right?" I muttered to myself.

Wait until Hawk gets back. See if they found any DNA. Stop jumping the gun. Assume nothing.

I grabbed my cold case file and flipped it open, then closed it again. *I can't do this now. I need to get some rest too. It's going to be a long day.*

I set the Mallard file aside, looked up at my almost empty whiteboard, shook my head, and went home.

6

It was just after five in the morning when I fell fully clothed on top of my bed. I think I must have been asleep even before my head hit the pillow. I woke four hours later at nine o'clock, feeling like death warmed over. I stripped off my clothes, staggered to the bathroom, turned on the shower, stepped into the cold water and almost died from the shock of it. I counted slowly to ten then turned up the heat, reveling in the warm blanket of water.

I shampooed my hair and then stepped out into the cold air of the bathroom, and I shivered, caught sight of myself in the mirror and wondered who the hell was the witch glaring back at me. *You're the one who wanted to switch to days,* I reminded myself.

I dried off, wrapped myself in a towel and went to the kitchen. Two minutes later I was seated, still wrapped in my towel, at the breakfast bar, sipping on a cup of steaming black coffee. *Thank you, Mr. Keurig, if that's what your name is.*

And suddenly I felt better... no, I felt great. I would have loved to have gone for a short run, but time was passing and I had a job to do. And I was hungry. I dressed quickly, gathered my bits and pieces together, and headed out into the wintery sunshine; it was nine-forty-five.

I stopped only to get coffee and an egg and sausage sandwich at the Bagel Shop and was in my office at the crack of ten o'clock. Janet was already there waiting for me. *Why am I not surprised?*

"Good morning, Janet," I said. "Where is everybody?"

"Ann and Lennie are getting coffee. They should be here soon."

"What about Hawk?"

"He didn't get to go home. He's still with Mike Willis processing Logan's car."

"Damn, I was hoping they'd be done. Oh never mind. Maybe they found something... or not," I said, gloomily. "Look, I have a couple of things I need to do... and I really don't want to get started on this thing until I know what, if anything, Forensics found in the car. So, why don't you and Ann run on over and talk to Logan's co-workers and see if they can add anything—friends with issues, enemies, affairs. You know the drill. I don't have to tell you how to do your jobs. Be back here by noon and we'll take it from there, okay?"

"What about Lennie?" Janet asked.

"Don't worry about him. I have a job for him to do while we're waiting for Hawk."

And she left, not looking too happy, but she left.

Me? I grabbed the cold case file, didn't I?

Poor Cappy T. Mallard. I looked first at the photos. Like

Logan, he'd been found in his car. And, also like Logan, his body was in the passenger seat, but it was folded over on itself and slumped over the center console onto the driver's seat. He, too, had been shot in the left temple. And, according to the medical examiner's report, he'd also been shot in the back of the head. Mallard's blood-alcohol level was 0.19, more than twice the legal limit.

So... I thought. *He was legally drunk, unfit to drive. If someone was driving him home...*

I scanned quickly through the remaining pages of the report, looking for more similarities and differences in the two cases. A nine-millimeter handgun was the probable murder weapon in both cases. The time of death was much later for Cappy, but that was about it.

Then my heart jumped at something curious when I saw the signature. It wasn't Doc's. The name on the report was that of a Doctor Terrance Boddinger, ME.

I grabbed my phone and called Doc's office.

"Medical examiner," Doc answered.

"Hey, Doc. It's me, Kate."

"No, absolutely not. I will not leave my wife for you no matter how much you beg," he said loudly.

I grinned. Same old same old.

"Tell Sophie I say hello and that she should quit bringing your lunch this early; it's not yet ten-thirty."

Every time I called when Doc's wife was around, that was how he answered the phone. I'd love to have Chief Johnston call from my phone and see what his reaction would be.

"It's not lunch," he said. "It's breakfast. I have not yet been home since you darkened my lab at midnight. Now, what d'you want? My sausage, bacon, and egg biscuit is getting cold."

"I want to know why you didn't do the autopsy on a Cappy T. Mallard on September 3, 2013?"

"Are you serious? That's more than four years ago. I can't remember that far back... September 3, 2013, you say? Hold on, Sophie's saying something... Apparently, I was on vacation. Sophie and I took a cruise around Sicily. We were gone for twelve days. I remember now. I came home with Montezuma's revenge, and I had jet lag for a month."

"Montezuma's revenge? What the hell is that?"

"An upset stomach would be the polite way to describe it."

"Oh, I see," I said, and I did, and I decided to pursue the subject no further. "Doc, are you sure, about the date? You don't need to check your calendar to make sure?" I asked.

"*Excuse me?*" he said.

Whoops, wrong question, but...

"Come on, Doc," I said soothingly, "you know I have to ask."

He sighed. "We were on a boat," he said with an edge to his voice. "I can send you Sophie's scrapbook, if you like. It has a dozen pictures of me in a swimsuit."

I shuddered at the thought of Doc in a swimsuit.

"Okay, I believe Sophie. So, do you have Doctor Boddinger's contact information? What d'you know about him, by the way? What's he like?"

"Kate, I am eating my breakfast, but since you obviously want me to starve, and because you always want your information *immediately*, and even though the law entitles me to eat now and then—"

"You can text it to me, Doc," I replied hopefully, inter-rupting him.

"Of course I can. Well, Sophie can... Sophie, will you send this information to Kate from your phone? Just the address and phone number... Dear, you know I hate texting. It always comes out wrong. You're the only one who can do it right. No, not because my fingers are too fat... Kate, are you still there?"

"Yes, Doc," I whispered, shaking my head.

"Sophie is sending it to you right now."

Doc's wife took care of him and kept him in line at the same time. I couldn't help but chuckle as I thanked Doc for his help and cooperation. He grunted something unintelli-gible and hung up on me without saying good-bye. I wasn't a bit put out. He did it all the time.

Sophie's text came through a few seconds later, word perfect; again, I had to smile. *What the hell would he do without her, I wonder?*

"So," I muttered, "Doctor Boddinger. I'm going to need to talk to you, but not right now." I made a note of his phone number and address and set it aside.

I knew that if Doc had worked on Cappy Mallard, he would have remembered it and made at least a comment about the similarities of the two cases during his examina-tion of Jack Logan. I wondered if Boddinger would remember the case.

I stared at the Mallard murder book, flipped through the pages, looking at them, but not seeing them, lost in thought; what if... *No, surely not!*

And then, on a whim, or maybe it was that divine guid-ance coaxing me along again, I put out a request to my brothers-in-blue across the tri-state area. I sent my request to all jurisdictions as far as and including Nashville, Knoxville, the Tri-Cities, Huntsville, Alabama, and finally to Atlanta. Several hundred departments in all, and then I wondered if I hadn't over-reached. But no, if any of them had open cases that fit my MO, I would hear about it. A forlorn hope? Yes, but in my game, hope is often all you have. Whatever, I figured it was worth a try.

After all, a man gets shot and left in his car on a deserted road; that was hardly a distinctive calling card, right? It happens all the time, right? *No, not as often as you might think...What the hell am I doing opening up this can of worms?*

Was I having second thoughts? You bet, but I'd learned a long time ago, from a man I still liked to call my friend, to go with my gut. Yes, it was a hunch. The chances of this Cappy T. Mallard case sticking in the back of my head for all these years only to resurface today was a mystery all its own. The urge to tie the two cases together was something I couldn't explain. I just had to go with it.

So, I fetched myself a second cup of coffee and settled down to wait. And, wouldn't you know it? I didn't have to wait long.

7

I spent the next hour working through Cappy's case file. The lead detective, a Sergeant Paul Hicks, a guy I knew quite well, which is probably why I remembered the case... Anyway, he'd chalked it up to the work of some drifter, maybe a drunken argument gone wrong. It was his last case before retirement, so it probably didn't get the attention that it deserved.

Cappy had no family. He was, so the report said, just a guy who was in the wrong place at the wrong time and met up with the wrong guy, or guys.

Yeah, right! I thought. *Time to call the good doctor, I think.*

I dialed the number Doc had given me and waited for Boddinger to answer, and I waited, and I was just about to give up when there was a click and a stern voice said, "Who is this?"

"I'm a police officer. Is this Doctor Terrence Boddinger?"

"It is. Please properly identify yourself."

Sheesh, really?

So I identified myself and then said, "Doctor, I'm investigating a homicide that took place here in Chattanooga last night. There are similarities between my victim and the death of a Mr. Cappy T. Mallard some five years ago, and I think the two cases might be connected. I see from the autopsy report that you did the post. Do you think we could meet to discuss it?"

"I doubt that very much, Detective." He sounded annoyed. "I have a full schedule all the way through until Christmas."

"You do understand that I'm conducting a homicide investigation, perhaps more than one?" I said. "You were the pathologist filling in for our regular medical examiner, Doctor Richard Sheddon. I really would appreciate your help, sir."

"Oh, I see. You think I, as an outsider, forgot to cross a "T" or dot an "I" and you feel a need to question my work? I can assure you, Detective, that my skills meet, if not exceed, those of your... regular ME."

What the hell is this guy talking about?

"Doctor Boddinger, no one is questioning your findings, just the opposite, in fact. As far as I can tell, everything is in order. I was hoping to discuss the case with you on a hunch that the two cases might be connected. You *do* understand two men are dead, and that Mallard's killer is still out there somewhere?"

"Detective, I understand your position, but you need to understand mine... Yes, I did the autopsy. It was, as I recall, an unremarkable case. I'm sure if there was anything unusual, I would have mentioned it in my report."

"Doctor Boddinger, I understand when you say that you're extremely busy, and I also understand that you might not be able to remember everything about an autopsy you did five years ago." I felt my chest tightening as I choked back the urge to start shouting. I was tired and aggravated by the man's attitude. "That's why I'd like to go over the file with you and have you look—"

"I remember it perfectly," he snapped, interrupting me. "Cappy T. Mallard was a transient, a visitor, passing through, from somewhere in Ohio, as I remember. He was a loner and more than likely fell in with the wrong person who robbed him and then killed him. It happens all the time. I'm sure I don't have to tell you that, Detective."

"Doctor Boddinger, you do know that if you don't comply with my request, I can have you picked up and brought in for questioning?"

"I don't like your tone, Detective. You can be sure I'll talk to your captain when I file a formal complaint. I've more things to worry about than the death of a bum more than four years ago. Now, if you don't mind, I have a speaking engagement before the Chattanooga Society of Physicians. I am also a close friend of the current Mayor."

"First of all, Doctor, I *am* Captain. Second, when you file your complaint, you'll want to talk to Chief Johnston," I said calmly. "Third, I don't give a damn who you know or where you have a speaking engagement. I'll have a unit waiting to pick you up when you return. Fourth, I'm sure the press will be interested to know that you're refusing to cooperate in a murder investigation, but hey, any publicity is good publicity, right?"

He clicked his tongue and muttered something. This

was the kind of guy who would call the police because a lunatic broke into his house, then sue the department after they saved his life because they damaged a vase in the process.

He was quiet for a moment then said, curtly, "One moment, please."

I heard him walking through his house, then I heard a door shut, and then a file cabinet open and slam shut. He must have put the phone down on his desk because I heard pages being flipped. There was an interruption when someone came to his door. It was a female voice asking a question I didn't quite catch.

"I'm on the phone!" he snapped, and I heard no more of the female voice.

"Are you there, Detective?"

"Yes, I'm still here."

"Mallard, Cappy T. He was forty-eight years old. Died of two gunshot wounds to the head. One entry point at the left temple. This I believed to be the first of the two wounds. The other at the base of the skull. There was also a bruise to his right thigh I never established had anything to do with his death. He had a blood-alcohol level of zero-point one-nine, more than twice the legal limit. You see? It was as I clearly stated. It's my considered opinion that this was nothing more than a robbery gone bad."

"Yes, I know, Doctor. All of that's in the file. But didn't you think it odd that after the assailant shot Mallard in the temple, someone in the back seat shot him again in the back of the head?"

"Detective, every case of murder is odd," he said, sounding bored.

It had become obvious that I wasn't going to have a worthwhile discussion about the oddities of Cappy T. Mallard's murder with Doctor Boddinger.

"You don't remember anything else? Nothing outstanding?" I asked without much hope in my voice.

"No," Boddinger said. "Detective... you and I both know that sometimes people get killed because they make stupid decisions. Mallard was one of those people. He had too much to drink and thought he could trust the person he allowed to drive him... to wherever it was he was staying."

So, you think he let someone drive him home too? That's interesting.

"That's what you think?" I asked.

"I do. He was legally drunk and likely chatting with someone at the bar. People who drink too much often make bad choices; you know that, Detective. It's the scenario that makes the most sense. Someone sees he's intoxicated, starts a conversation with him, and offers to drive him home with the intention of robbing him. The next thing you know, the man sobers up at the last minute and by then it's too late. The viper has already slithered up your pant leg, so to speak."

He's right, of course, I thought. *But still... Maybe they didn't intend to kill him, but simply intended to rob him and take his car; they sure as hell weren't going to walk back to town... And now there were two murders, at least. Could it be that there are two predators targeting the local bars? Geez, if the press gets hold of it they'll have a field day.*

"Detective? Detective Gazzara, are you still on the line?" he snapped.

"Yes, uh... yes. Sorry, Doctor."

"Look, if you really insist on carrying on with this conversation, I must ask that we continue at another time. If not, I'll be late to my speaking engagement."

"No. I think I have enough, for now anyway. You've been very helpful; thank you... I would remind you, however, that the investigation is ongoing, and I may have to contact you again."

He didn't answer.

"I appreciate your assistance, Doctor."

He hung up without saying goodbye. *Hmm, are all doctors like that, I wonder?*

I sighed, stared at the iPhone screen, shook my head, dropped the phone onto my desktop, then leaned back in my chair, linked my fingers together at the back of my head, closed my eyes, and thought back over my conversation with the good doctor. Unfortunately, that didn't get me anywhere new, except more irritated at the doctor's arrogance.

I let my chair fall forward, set my elbows on my desktop, my hands over my ears, and I stared up at the whiteboard and my half-dozen cell phone photos of Jack Logan's body.

"You're jumping the gun, Kate," I mumbled. "Two murders do not a serial killer make. Three are required before we can call it that. Follow the trail and see where it leads."

I sat up straight, opened my laptop, and began to read through my emails...

I t was the last email in my inbox, the one that set my world on fire. Even before I opened it, my instincts told me life was about to get harder. Why else would I be receiving an email from Sheriff Lyndon Cane in Dalton, Georgia?

The subject line read: *Regarding your cold case request.*

In a nutshell, Sheriff Cane was more than happy to share the details of a cold case that had stumped him for more than four years.

I sighed and wrote down his contact information, intending to call him as soon as I could get my act together. Even so, I couldn't help but wonder if I now had a third victim. I hoped not... but deep down, somewhere in the depths of my soul, I also hoped that it was. Then again, I wondered if maybe I was seeing ghosts and specters where there were none, where there was nothing but shadows? I needed to bring in my team; get some input, second opinions.

I shook off the feeling of impending doom and began to make a list of what needed to be done.

First, I had to track down Jack Logan's ex-wife. If she had anything to do with his death, I could put my case to bed and forget Cappy and Sheriff Cane. It would also put to rest the tiny voice inside my head that kept telling me, *Kate, you've got a pattern killer here. Hunting season on middle-aged men is open.*

Second, I needed to get a hold of Hawk. He was working with Mike Willis's forensics team; they were still processing Logan's car.

I reached for my desk phone to call him, but before my fingers hit the handset, all hell broke loose.

There was a beep and my message light started blinking. I picked up and tapped in my code. An electronic, female voice informed me that I had five messages. That wasn't unusual, and neither were the first two messages: they were run-of-the-mill demands for overdue paperwork. The third message, however, was a punch in the gut. Sheriff Pete McGraw from Huntsville, Alabama, informed me, in a voice that sounded like gravel, that he had a cold case that matched my description.

I swallowed hard. I needed more coffee in the worst way. Even the crap in the situation room would help. I grabbed my to-go mug from the credenza and headed out, returning a few minutes later. I hadn't been seated more than a minute when there was a knock on the door and Janet, Ann, and Lennie stepped inside.

"We have news for you, Cap," Ann said.

"Sit down, all of you, round the table. We need to talk. Has anyone heard from Hawk? Any news on the car?"

"I called him last night, but it went to voicemail," Ann said as she sat down. "He texted me back that he'd be in today, but he didn't say when."

"Damn," I muttered. "Fine. So what's the news?"

"We, the three of us, have been doing research and interviews. A few months ago, Logan's current wife took out a restraining order on the ex-wife. It's good for a year," Ann said. "And someone called Lester Harris also took one out on the ex-wife six months ago; it's still good, too."

"Really, that's interesting, but just hold that thought for a minute. I have some bad news."

I stood, grabbed my coffee, stepped around my desk, and took a seat at the table between Ann and Miller.

"On a hunch I did a little digging," I said. And then I explained finding the Cappy Mallard cold case, sending out the email for a tri-state search, and the responses I'd received so far.

"So... that's four then," Miller said hesitantly. "You're thinking that we have a serial killer?"

Miller was one of those happy individuals who always seemed to be smiling, but having said the dreaded words, he looked as if he'd just seen a ghost.

"It's too soon to say," I replied. "Right now we have two victims; both died in a similar manner. We have two more possibles, but until I've talked to the two sheriffs, we can't assume anything. Yes, I have a hunch, but that's all it is. Right now, other than the similarities of these first two cases, we've nothing to go on."

It was true, but deep down, I was convinced. A hunch? I'd rather call it intuition: I had a feeling that we were going to be in for a long haul, that nothing was going to come easy.

And after everything was said and done, I was almost certain we were looking for a predator, maybe two.

"Do you still want us to interview the ex-wife?" Janet asked.

"Yes. We need to eliminate her... or not," I said. "Not would be good. If she killed her ex-husband or paid someone to kill him, it would be over and done with; we could put it to bed. You and I, Janet, will go pay her a visit later. Miller, how about the bars and restaurants in the area around the three towers, what did you find?"

"Unfortunately, there are plenty of options. There's a string of eleven bars—some of them just holes-in-the-wall— several restaurants, mostly small BBQ joints and the like, and there's an Applebee's. There's also a handful of carry-outs."

"Okay, you and Ann start canvasing the area. Start with those that have security cameras. Take Jack Logan's photo with you. See if anyone remembers seeing him."

There was a tap on the door. It opened and Hawk entered.

"Hawk," I said with mock surprise. "How nice of you to join us. How was your vacation?" I said, waving him to a seat at the table.

Sergeant Arthur "Hawk" Hawkins, the third member of my small team—there were five of us, including me—was sixty-four years old. He'd been a detective for twenty-nine years and had less than a year left to go before retirement. I used to think he'd been transferred to me so that he could work out the rest of his term in relative peace, but on reflection, I think the Chief was making sure I had what I needed to get the job done. Hawk was not a huge team player, but a real asset nonetheless.

He was a handsome man, five-ten, a little overweight at two hundred ten pounds, clean-shaven, with white hair, piercing blue eyes, a sharp nose, sunburned face. I'd known him a long time, too. He came across as a tough old man, but his heart was big and soft.

He nodded, sat down, looked stone-faced at everyone, then said, "You know what I've been doing. I've spent the last eighteen hours with Willis and his team processing our victim's freakin' car."

"And?" I said.

He reached into his inside pocket and pulled out a worn notebook, flipped through the pages, and cleared his throat.

Janet looked at me and I knew what she was thinking. *How come he gets to use a paper notebook?* A couple years ago when she'd started as my partner, I made her give up her paper notebooks for an iPad.

"It's not a frickin' novel, Hawk. Just spill it," Ann said.

"Just cool your jets, Robar," he said, staring at his notes. "Okay, we did recover a bullet fragment on the dash. Willis thinks it was from the shot through the base of the skull that shattered the windshield. He's not sure, but he thinks it's a frangible."

Hawk looked at Janet, and said, "For those of you that might not know, frangible bullets are designed to break apart, to fragment on impact. That, however, doesn't always happen. The earliest versions can still go clean through a person, and even a wall, because the bullet will not always break apart and release its energy inside its intended target."

Janet's fair skin was flushed, but she listened and gave Hawk a single nod when he finished.

He flipped another page, then continued, "There were several medium-length blond hairs on the driver's headrest, obviously out of a bottle—according to Willis—and obviously not the victim's. We found plenty more, most of which probably belonged to the victim, Logan. We may get some DNA from those. And there were some brunette hairs that probably belonged to the wife. Mike's running them through the system as we speak. We also found a Band-Aid, a small one, on the floor in the back, but under the passenger seat. He's working that too, but it will take a while; always does."

"Do we know what color the ex-wife's hair is?" I asked. They all shook their heads.

"Well, Janet," I said, "you and I will soon find out. If she's a bottle blond, she goes to the head of the suspect list. Since Sherri Logan has taken out a restraining order against her, seems the ex-wife might have a temper... What else, Hawk?"

He stared at his notes.

"Fingerprints?" Janet asked.

"Oh yeah, plenty. They are being processed, but I'm afraid, they're just those of the victim and, we assume his wife... We're assuming that because there are a lot of them, all over the car. We'll need prints from her and the ex for comparison."

I nodded. "We'll get the ex's this afternoon. Ann, you and Lennie go get them from..." I glanced up at the board, "from Sherri Logan. Get a swab from her too, turn them in to Willis, then start making the rounds of the bars. What are your plans for the rest of the day, Hawk? You probably should go home and get some rest."

He shook his head. "Nah, it's too early for me. Look, Willis hasn't yet been able to properly process the scene; it was too dark last night, and he's heading that way in..." he checked his watch. "Well, as we speak. I thought I'd go with him, snoop around a little, if that's okay with you, Cap."

"Good idea. They had to have left the scene somehow, probably on foot... unless there was a third person with them." I shuddered at the thought. "So yes, go ahead."

And before I could say another word, he was on his feet and heading toward the door.

I looked at the rest of my team and said, "Let's go to it," and they too upped and left the room, all except Janet, who remained seated, searching through her own notes on her iPad.

"Something on your mind?" I asked.

"This one is a real mystery. I hate to use the term. But I'm coming up with nothing. No ideas. No guesses. Nothing. It's like someone just leaned into Jack Logan's car, shot him in the head, and took his money."

"No," I shook my head. "There's more to it than that. They didn't lean into his car. He was in the passenger seat, which means someone else was driving. Go grab Hawk and bring him back. I need to ask him a question."

Janet returned with Hawk a few minutes later.

"You summoned?" he said.

"Hey," I said. "The driver's seat, how was it positioned? Had it been moved during the crime, d'you think?"

He shrugged. "Hard to tell. Mike Willis removed it. You'll have to ask him."

I nodded, disappointed. "Okay. Check-in with me when you get back."

"You got it, Cap."

He left and I said to Janet, "I need to talk to Mike, then we'll go talk to the ex-wife. It should be fun. I hear she's a real sweetheart."

9

M ike Willis confirmed that both seats were not in an unusual position. In fact, had he not been found in the passenger seat, Jack Logan might well have been driving.

I listened to what he had to say, asked a few questions, made an appointment to visit with him later the following morning, then we headed out to beard the lioness in her den.

It was just after three o'clock that Wednesday afternoon when we arrived at Cynthia Logan's home. I hadn't called ahead, wanting to retain an element of surprise. It's a tool that almost always works in our favor.

I already knew that the house was a rental, set in a quiet, middle-class neighborhood; what I didn't expect was the size of the home, and the sparkling new Ford truck parked in the driveway.

I had a job, no kids, and could comfortably afford a one-bedroom apartment and a used Toyota, so I figured it was a pretty nice set-up for a woman who, according to court divorce records, was singing the blues about her finances.

As we approached the front door, we could hear music playing inside, the kind of music you hear at carnivals on rides called The Barn Burner or The Cyclone. It wasn't loud enough to disturb the neighbors, but it was loud enough to be heard as we stepped up the porch steps. I knocked on the door hard enough for it to be heard over the music. A few seconds later, the door opened and Cynthia Logan took one look at us, then shook her head and laughed out loud.

"Sooner than I thought," she said. "I knew it was only a matter of time before you showed up on my doorstep. My but you're quick."

Hmm, the lady has blond hair. Just the right length, too.

"Quick?" I asked. "You're Jack Logan's ex-wife. He's dead. His current wife has a restraining order against you. So quick? Yes. What else would you expect, Ms. Logan?"

I introduced Janet and myself, flashing my badge and identification. I had a certain feeling this woman knew just enough about the rules of the game and that if I didn't follow them to the letter I would indeed be facing an Internal Affairs investigation.

"May we come in, Ms. Logan?"

"So you're here to talk to me about that idiot I married. Well, I didn't kill him." She made no effort to let us in. Instead, she folded her arms across her chest defiantly and shifted from her right foot to her left.

"We didn't say you did, Miss Logan," Janet said with a smile.

"Call me Cynthia." Her snarky tone made it clear she wasn't happy we were there.

I thought for a minute that she was going to make us conduct the interview on the front step, if at all, but then she relented, her voice softened as she said, "Yes, fine, come on in."

We followed her into the living room. The music was coming from a small, somewhat aged boombox with a CD player. It was set next to a large flat-screen television. An open laptop on the table was showing one of those social media sites where people post every move of every day, make connections, hookups, and argue about politics.

Me? I have a love/hate relationship with social media. On the one hand, I hate it because of the phoniness of it all, the lies, the subterfuge, the photos people post of themselves. But I love it when the geniuses on the other side of the law post their wrongdoings with live footage of their crimes. Dumb? Yes, I know, but it happens more often than you think. It's law enforcement's secret weapon, and it isn't even a secret.

Janet was ahead of me and I knew she'd also spotted the open laptop; so did Cynthia, because she quickly slammed it shut. I smiled, because there was nothing she could do about the joint smoldering in an ashtray next to it.

"It's for medicinal purposes," she said as she pinched it out and moved the ashtray to the mantlepiece. "I have a license."

"I don't care what you're smoking, Ms. Logan. I'm here to talk to you about your ex-husband."

She shook her head, smirked and said, "You know, that asshole died owing me more than fifty thousand dollars."

She waited for a response but got none.

"That was the least of what I gave him over the course of our marriage," she continued. "Then he ditches me and marries that whore, Sherri, and leaves me holding the bag."

"Holding the bag for what?" I asked.

"All of my medical expenses, of course." She clicked her tongue and slowly eased herself down into a leather recliner.

"Sit down," she said, "wherever you like."

Janet and I sat down together on a couch that must have set her back a couple of grand. I opened my purse and took out a small digital recorder and turned it on.

"I'm going to record our conversation, Ms. Logan. Do I have your permission?"

She looked at the recorder as if it were a cobra readying itself to strike. I thought for a minute that she was going to refuse, but she didn't; she nodded, reluctantly.

"Out loud, for the record, please, Ms. Logan."

"Yes, okay, fine."

"So, you mentioned medical expenses," I said, setting the tiny machine down in front of her on the coffee table.

"Yes, I suffer from depression and have back problems."

"Do you work?" I asked, already knowing the answer.

"Not anymore. I can't. Some days I just can't bear to get out of bed. I can't hold a regular job so money is tight. I'm on disability. I barely get by, but d'you think that son-of-a-bitch would help me out? Nope. Not one red cent."

She ran her hand through her hair. She didn't look at all depressed. She looked pissed off. Her eyes were blue and almost completely concealed when she smirked, which seemed to be just about all the time. Her face was heavily wrinkled, leathery from years of overexposure to the sun. Her hair was blond, not quite shoulder length, and the roots were showing. She was wearing jeans and a tight T-shirt that made it painfully obvious that she had implants that had increased her breast size by at least two cups. She was also wearing three thin gold bracelets around each of her wrists and another around her left ankle.

"So, Ms. Logan," I said, "you and Jack divorced in 2003; fifteen years ago. That's a long time... How did you meet him, by the way?"

She ran her hand through her hair again and let her hand slap on her thigh. "We met at a bar. If you can believe that."

I certainly could, but I didn't say anything.

"He always loved sports," she said thoughtfully. "You know, baseball, football, basketball. I wasn't interested... in sports, but he seemed nice, and he bought me drinks, so I started seeing him. We'd usually meet at a sports bar and go on from there. He was lonely, and kinda sad-looking. I sort of felt like... sorry for him, you know? He was a Cubs fan; the Braves, too."

She smirked. "But he was actually a lot of fun. Not a party animal, but he'd walk me to my car after the game was over, and sometimes he'd bring me a little present like this." She picked out one of the delicate little bracelets around her wrist with her pink manicured nails.

"How long did you date before you got married?" I asked.

"Three months," she snapped, looking at me as if daring me to say something snarky.

I obliged.

"A whirlwind romance, then?"

"That's right. We went to the Grand Canyon for our honeymoon and spent a few days in Vegas. I remember I won four-hundred-and-eighteen dollars." She lifted her chin as if we'd all be impressed. "Jack didn't win anything. He didn't even bet. Then, once we were married, he changed, and it was like pulling teeth trying to get a dime out of him."

"How long did you stay married?" I asked.

"Four years."

"Jack wasn't your first husband, was he?" I asked.

"I was married before, yes." She rolled her eyes. "The first time when I was eighteen... Sam was twenty. That lasted almost four years. Then again when I was twenty-nine, to Ray Watson. That lasted until..."

"That lasted until you met Jack," I said.

All the while I was talking to her, Janet was doing what she did best. She was slowly, carefully taking in the scenery and putting together a profile in her head as she listened to us talk.

"Yes, two years, give or take. I left Ray to be with Jack. But Jack didn't know that, of course." She shifted in her seat. "My marriage to Ray was over. He cheated on me with someone I knew. At least I had the decency to find a stranger."

I couldn't help but note that she was actually proud that her cheating standards were a fraction of an inch higher than those of her second husband.

"So, you were what, thirty-three when you married Jack in 1999?"

"Yes, that's right."

"And Jack would have been... thirty-four?"

She nodded.

"And you expected life with Jack to be different?" I asked.

"Yeah, of course I did. He had more money, a steady job: he was an accountant, you know. I was supposed to be taken care of. That was what he was always saying. That he was going to take care of me. But I still had to keep working. I still had to do everything around the house. It wasn't fair."

Her eyes widened as she looked for a nod or smirk of approval from me. She got neither.

"If anyone should have been asking for a divorce, it should have been me. I had more reasons than that son-of-a-bitch. And then he goes and marries that whore. She's driving around in a Cadillac, you know. A freaking Cadillac for God's sake!"

"Is that your truck out there?" I jerked my thumb toward the window. "I wouldn't say that was a beater."

She blushed, probably for the first time in a long time. "That's not mine. I'm just borrowing it from a friend. I had some errands to run."

"Ms. Logan, we know that Sherri Logan took out a restraining—"

She cut me off quickly. "Yeah, a restraining order. I know. She didn't want me contacting him when I needed help." She raised her right eyebrow, and said, "He wouldn't answer his phone, damn it. I had no choice but to show up at their house."

"Why would you do that?" Janet asked. "He filed for the divorce. Not you. Why would you want to stay in contact? You have no children, not even a pet to share."

"Look, I know our marriage wasn't perfect, but he led

me to believe... swore to me that we were going to be together until death do us part." She pointed at Janet. "He made it so I came to rely on certain things, and then he took it all away. He *owed* me."

"What about Lester Harris, what does he owe you?" I asked. "He has a restraining order out on you, too. What's that all about?"

"Lester Harris..." she stuttered. "That was... is... Look, I threatened to take out a restraining order on him, so he beat me to it; he took one out on me first... to make me look bad. He's been stalking me, you know. We went out on a couple of dates and now he thinks he owns me. I think he could be dangerous. In fact, I wouldn't be surprised if he did something to Jack just to get at me. He's that kind of crazy."

"If he's that dangerous, why didn't you get a restraining order immediately?" I asked. I have to admit I was enjoying watching her back herself into a corner.

"I had hopes for Lester, at first, but... well, I was wrong. I thought if I just showed him some kindness, he'd leave me alone." She sniffled. Was she really trying to cry in front of us? "No good deed goes unpunished, right?" she said.

"Where were you between the hours of five and six o'clock on the evening Jack was killed?" I asked.

"Oh hey. Here it comes," she said. Her sniffles quickly disappeared and her tone turned angry. There was no doubt that she believed that she was a victim, the victim of a cruel and vindictive ex-husband. *And there's your motive.*

"Where were you, Ms. Logan?" I asked again.

"You know, you people have a lot of nerve coming after me," she snarled. "There are rapists and murderers out there and—"

"And one of them got your ex-husband," Janet snapped. "Now tell us where you were."

"I don't remember," Cynthia said, biting her lip.

"What do you mean you don't remember?" I said, rolling my eyes.

"I was here till... Oh, I don't know... maybe eight o'clock. No, there was no one here with me. Then I went out to a bar. I met a guy. He bought me a drink... and that's the last I remember until I woke up in my car... in a damn ditch. You can check. My car's at the collision center on Rossville Boulevard. The damn front end is shoved in. Luckily, I have insurance, but my shoes were gone, so was my cash. The bastard must have drugged me." She jerked her chin toward the front window. "That's why I have the truck. I borrowed it from the woman who does my nails."

"We're in the wrong business," Janet said, looking up at me, wiggling her fingers, and then rising to her feet.

I stared at the woman, not knowing what to make of her so-called alibi that wasn't an alibi at all. She was at home, so she said, when her ex-husband was killed, but was she? Was all that stuff about her being drugged just so much BS? Oh, there was no doubt we'd find her car was indeed involved in a wreck when she said it was, but drugged? Maybe, maybe not.

"This man you met," I said, "can you describe him? What was his name?"

"He said his name was Will something. He was kinda small, maybe five-nine, nicely dressed, good-looking... That's all I remember. I was only with him for about thirty minutes."

"What about the bar?" Janet asked.

"Roper's Sports Bar on Battlefield Parkway. Look, I know what you're thinking, but you're wrong. I didn't kill Jack. If I was gonna kill anyone... and I wasn't, it would have been that stupid little woman he married, not him."

"Can you think of anyone who might have wanted to hurt Jack?" Janet asked. "Did he have any enemies?"

"No, not that I know of. Well, um, like I said, Lester Harris, maybe. He's obsessed with me. Maybe he thought Jack and I were getting back together or something, and—"

"Where would he have gotten an idea like that?" I asked. I was beginning to understand this bitter, self-victimized woman. I'd seen it before, more often than I cared to admit. She loved attention, was addicted to it. And I knew exactly what was coming next.

"I don't know," she snapped, pulling her shoulders up to her ears. "Maybe I said something. I might have told him that Jack still loved me," she said, her eyes lowered.

Yes, of course you did.

"Did you still love Jack?" I asked.

"I loved his money." She tried to smile cutely, then giggled, like a flirting teenager. More play-acting, but it didn't work. It was pathetic, and I didn't like Cynthia Logan, not one bit. I decided to change tactics.

"Have you ever been to Huntsville, Alabama? Or Dalton, Georgia?" I asked, looking down at my notes.

"Dalton, of course I have, many times. I've been all over," she bragged.

"You've been to both cities? When?" I asked.

"Dalton? Dozens of times, mostly to the outlet mall. The last time... I don't know. A couple of months ago, maybe? Huntsville? Oh, it has to have been a couple of years ago. Just a short getaway, in the spring as I recall, May, I think it was. A change of scenery. They say that's as good as a rest, don't they?" She nodded. "I've also been to Colorado, Wyoming, California, Wisconsin, New York, Washington, and... lots of places."

I made a note of everything she said, but I knew I didn't dare reach out to those states at this early stage in the investigation. What I did know was that things weren't looking good for Cynthia Logan. The fact that she'd visited Dalton was inconsequential; I'd visited Dalton many times myself, and for the same reasons she had. That she'd also visited Huntsville, well, that was something, but coincidental and circumstantial, and I wouldn't know better until I'd spoken to Sheriff McGraw.

I had nothing solid, and I felt like I was trying to put a set of cuffs around the steam coming out of a kettle.

"Miss Logan," Janet said, conversationally. "Lester Harris said you showed up at his house and threw rocks through three of his windows, and that you also threatened to kill his dog and then him. Was that before or after you told him you were going to file a restraining order against him?"

"Look, that was a mistake. I had had one too many drinks. I'll admit that. I'm not perfect. Who hasn't let the alcohol do the talking for them at one time or another?"

She was right, but most people don't resort to throwing rocks and making threats.

"You didn't just talk, Cynthia. You threw rocks and threatened him and his dog," Janet continued. "It seems to me that you have a bit of a temper?"

"Well, I've been through a lot. It's only natural," she

said matter-of-factly as if we were supposed to smack our foreheads with our palms, nod our heads and say 'oh, well, that explains it then.'

"Does that mean yes, you have a temper?" Janet was like a dog with a bone.

"Oh, come on, nobody likes to be jerked around, do they? Or maybe you do. You look like one of those stupid young girls that believe in happily-ever-after," she said, staring at Janet.

"That's enough, Ms. Logan," I said. "I think we've taken up enough of your time." I stood and reached into my pocket for a business card. "If you can think of anything else that might help us, please give me a call."

She didn't make any effort to get up from her seat. I set the card down on the table and picked up my recorder, but I didn't turn it off.

"I didn't kill Jack, you know," she said, the smirk back on her face.

"You've made the point several times," I said.

"Do you mind if I use your bathroom?" Janet asked.

Cynthia rolled her eyes and let out a sigh and said, "If you must. It's down that hall on your left." She pointed. "I'll ask that you respect my privacy. I didn't see a search warrant with those badges."

"Of course. Thank you," Janet said and disappeared down the hall.

"I get the feeling you don't believe me," she said. "I know you've probably spoken to Jack's wife already, and I can just imagine what she had to say about me. She has a vivid imagination, so don't let that innocent act of hers fool you."

"What I believe isn't the issue here, Ms. Logan. I go where the evidence leads me. As they say on television, 'just the facts ma'am.'"

"So what did happen to Jack?" she asked. "Do you know if he had life insurance? I'm sure you do. You people have to look into that kind of thing, don't you? I'm sure Sherri had a hefty policy on him. She'll be laughing all the way to the bank; just you mark my words. A fricking Cadillac. Would you believe it?" She clicked her tongue, scowled, and shook her head, almost violently.

"I wouldn't know about any of that," I said.

The look on her face was pure evil. Was I looking at a killer? I didn't know, but one thing I was sure of was that her moral compass sure as hell wasn't pointing north.

Janet returned, adjusting her badge on her belt. Cynthia looked her up and down as if she suspected that she'd stolen a roll of toilet paper.

I stood up and said, "We'll be in touch, Ms. Logan. Thank you again for your time."

"I was thinking, Miss Logan," Janet said as we approached the front door. "Do you own a gun?"

"According to the Second Amendment, I am allowed to own as many as I want. But no. I used to have one. I don't know what happened to it. It got lost sometime after Jack and I got married." She stared at Janet. "But I think I should probably consider getting another one, don't you? Who knows, the person who killed Jack might come after me next."

"Boy, it must be tough having the whole world against you," Janet said sarcastically.

I'm going to have to talk to her, I thought. *She's going to get herself into trouble.*

"You're a real smart ass, aren't you?" Cynthia snapped back.

Janet chuckled, then stared at her and said, "Don't leave town, Miss Logan."

Oh... my God, I thought. *Really?*

I opened the front door and we stepped out onto the porch. The door slammed shut behind us. I turned off my recorder and said, "What the hell were you trying to do in there?"

"She's hiding something. I know she is. I was just trying to prod her a little, hoping she'd lose her temper; we know she's got one, right? D'you think she's really suffering from depression, or a back injury? I sure don't. And I'm certain she doesn't have a prescription for medical marijuana either. Oh yeah, she's bad, and... well, I guess we'll find out sooner or later."

"You're probably right," I said, "but you need to be careful who you're poking. You haven't had a brush with Internal Affairs yet, but what you did in there... well, she knows I was recording the interview, and if she makes an official complaint, you could be in for a wild ride. Tone it down a little, okay?"

"You think?"

"I do."

She nodded, but she didn't say she would. Instead, she said, "Oh, and did you notice her blond hair?" She pulled the car door closed.

"Yes, so?"

"Well, here you go," she said as she pulled a small plastic baggie from her pocket, grinning. "There was a hairbrush in her bathroom. I couldn't help myself. Maybe Mike Willis can find us a match."

10

Miller and Ann had still not returned when we arrived back at the PD. Janet went to find Hawk, and I went to get coffee. It was some ten minutes after I returned to my desk when Hawk came into my office.

"Hey, you," I said. "Did you talk to Janet?"

"Yeah. She gave me this." He waved the small baggie with a sample of Cynthia Logan's hair in it. "She asked me to give it to Mike for analysis. I'll do it on my way out. You got a minute, Cap?"

"Sure. What's up?"

He took up his usual spot on the corner of my desk. The knees of his pants were dirty like he'd been crawling around on the ground.

I raised my eyebrows and said, "You were going to the scene with Mike Willis. So, what have you got for me?"

"Mike got sidetracked. I went out there by myself," he said, smiling like I've never seen him smile before.

"Well, are you going to tell me, or do I have to rip out

your fingernails?"

"A bullet..."

"No shit," I said excitedly. "Where? How?"

"Don't get too excited. It's, well it's a partial, kinda flat, but I reckon there's enough to work with. It's a nine, looks like a range round, FMJ. Pretty common around here."

FMJ is the acronym for full metal jacket.

"So Doc was wrong when he said the killer was using frangible rounds?" I said. "That's another piece of luck. How the hell did you find it?"

"Yeah, the harder I work, the luckier I get. It's always there... somewhere. The perp always leaves something at the scene, or takes something away, or both. You just have to buckle down and look for it."

"Yes, I know; that's Forensics 101. So come on, Hawk, give."

"So I told you I was going out to the scene to snoop around. Thankfully, that road isn't traveled much," he said as he pulled a folded piece of paper from his pocket and handed it to me. It was a simple sketch of the scene.

"I'd spent hours with Willis processing the car and all we could come up with was a couple of hairs." He scratched at the stubble across his chin. "I knew I was missing something. I was literally banging my head against the hood of the car, trying to figure out what it was. Then it hit me like a ton of bricks. The window was rolled up."

"What do you mean?" I asked.

"It was one of those blatantly obvious clues that can get missed because we're so focused on looking for the small stuff." He shrugged, then continued, "See, Logan was shot in the side of the head first—"

"We don't know that," I said, interrupting him, "not for sure."

"Yeah, we do," he insisted. "It's the only thing that makes sense, especially when you know what I found. We saw an exit wound for both bullets. The second shot to the back of the head went out through the windshield and is lost forever, but the first shot..." He paused for dramatic effect. "It went out through the *open* passenger side window. Our perp rolled it up *after* shooting him."

"How d'you know that?" I asked.

"Because if the window had been closed, not only would there be blood and tissue all over it, the bullet would probably have shattered it. But see, there was none of that. The window was spotless except for along the very top where Logan's blood sprayed."

I stared at him. He grinned back at me. It made sense.

"So that's why you wanted to go to the scene?" I asked.

"Yeah, I had no hopes of finding the slug, but hey, stranger things, right? And this time, as you say, I got lucky. It wasn't easy. It's open country out there. The crime scene tapes are still there, and the tire marks, so I knew the exact position of the vehicle. Here, gimme that," he said, reaching for his map.

"See this?" He pointed to a small square to the east of the car. "It's an old barn. It's about... oh, maybe a hundred yards from the road. You wouldn't see it at night, not in the dark. Here..." He took his phone from his pocket. "I took photos. I found the bullet here, right at the northwest edge of the building; two more inches to the left and it would've been gone forever. Fortunately, that old barnwood is as hard as iron. This is where I found it in relationship to the car."

He pointed to his drawing and the dotted line that connected the car to the barn.

Hawk had an eye for details, and that's what made him a good detective. There was no disputing what he'd found, and he'd backed it up with the drawing and photos.

"I think maybe Logan tried to exit the vehicle while it was still moving, and that's what got him shot," Hawk said. "I'm not sure that spot was supposed to be his dumping ground, so I'm not going to speculate about that. So, Cap, what d'you think?"

"I think you did great," I said, shaking my head at my own understatement.

And I knew what he was getting at about where the car and body ended up. If Logan was being taken to another location, the perpetrator might have a place where he likes to dump the bodies. The thought of there being more bodies out there somewhere made my stomach flip.

Hawk continued, talking more than he had in months, "Here's the thing though. When I left here this morning, I wasn't really going looking for a bullet. I mean, what were the chances? No, what I was going after was footprints... See I figured there was only one way the perp, or perps, could have left the scene, and that was on foot. And that meant there was a possibility I might find prints, and I did. I found one about twenty yards south of where the car was discovered, right on the soft shoulder."

He paused and grinned at me, then continued, "I'm a size eleven. This one, a right foot, looks to be a nine, maybe nine and a half. I made a cast. Mike has it. See?" He showed me a photo of the cast on his iPhone; it had a yellow and black measure next to it. It looked to be about eleven inches long.

"That's kind of small, don't you think? Are you sure it's not the photographer's or one the techs?" I asked.

"Yeah. I already checked with forensics. None of them have this make of shoe or fit the size. It looks like it was made by a boot of some sort, by a small guy."

"So what do you have planned next?" I asked. "Janet is confirming the ex-wife's alibi." I gave Hawk the gory details of our visit with the lovely Cynthia Logan. "If her hairs match those you found at the scene, we at least know she was in his car."

"What about his wife?" Hawk asked. "Do we know the color of her hair?"

"I don't, but I'm sure Janet does. I'll check."

"I bet she's a brunette. We found plenty of those, and his. How long has Logan owned the car? If he had it before the divorce, his ex-wife's hair inside it means nothing."

"True, but—"

"And what if they don't match?" Hawk asked.

"Back to the drawing board. Come on, Hawk. You know the drill," I said and took a sip of my now cold coffee.

"Does she own a gun?" he asked.

"Said she lost it a while back," I replied.

"Of course she did. I'm not saying the woman did it, but she sounds just like every other bitter ex-wife. Hates the guy but not enough to kill him herself. So she pays some poor dope to do it," Hawk said as he slid off my desk.

"Is that what you think happened?" I asked.

"Yep."

"Simple as that?" I shook my head.

"Simple as that. I mean no disrespect, Cap, but women can be just as cruel and heartless as any man, even more so. Evil doesn't favor one sex over the other."

"You've got that right," I said, but my mind was on other things.

I checked my watch. It was almost three o'clock. "What are your plans now, Hawk?"

"I'm gonna take these to Mike." He held up the baggie with the hairs. "And then I'm going home. I've been on my feet for two days straight. I need some sleep."

"That you do. Okay, so, do me a favor on your way out. Tell Janet what your thoughts are about an accomplice, and then tell her to talk to this guy Lester Harris. He took out a restraining order on Cynthia Logan. That could all be smoke and mirrors. Then again, he might be able to tell us more about Cynthia."

Hawk nodded and headed out the door.

Me? I had some phone calls to make. The first of which was with Sheriff Lyndon Cane in Dalton. I tapped in his number and my call was answered by his secretary. I explained who I was and that Cane was expecting the call, and she put me through.

"Captain Gazzara," he said when he came on the line. "I've heard a lot about you. I wish we were talking under different circumstances."

"Yes, sir, me too," I said. "Thank you for your time. I have to tell you, though, that I wish this conversation wasn't happening at all. To be honest, when I sent out my request, I was hoping I wouldn't hear back from anyone. But here we are, and again, thank you for getting back to me. So, please tell me what you've got."

He was silent for a moment and I heard papers rustling, then he said, "Okay, Captain, the victim's name is Lawrence Berryman. Age forty-eight. Caucasian. Average height of five feet ten and one-half inches. He was a plumber. Married. Clean record. No priors. Cause of death, either one of two gunshot wounds to the head. One to the left temple, the other the base of the skull.

"He was found in his car at seven minutes after eight— that's the time the call came in—on Wednesday, November twenty-fifth, 2015, just outside the city limits on Cleveland Highway. He was in the passenger seat. Both bullets exited the head. The one to the back of the head exited the car through the windshield. The one to the left side of the head impacted the passenger side door frame. There was no way to tell which shot came first, but we assumed it was the one to the temple. It was fired from a distance of about eighteen inches, the one to the back of the head from less than two inches."

Sheriff Cane sighed and then said, "How does that compare to your victim?"

As I listened to him relate the details, with every word he spoke, my heart sank a little lower.

"I hate to say it," I said, "but it sounds identical. Would you mind FedExing a copy of the file to me, please?"

"Of course. I'll have Lily do it just as soon as we finish."

I nodded, even though I knew he couldn't see me, then said, "Anything else I should know, Sheriff? You said some-thing about the time the call came in. I'm assuming there was a delay between the time the body was found and the finder calling it in, right?"

"Yes, that's right. The car might have remained undiscovered longer but for a guy by the name of Michael Hartwell. Apparently, he was heading home after an office Thanksgiving party in Cleveland, Tennessee. I think he may have had a little too much to drink, though he wasn't charged. Be that as it may, he had to pull over to take a leak..."

The Sheriff cleared his throat. "Er, sorry, Captain. Anyway, he pulled over and stepped just far enough off the road into the woods to have a little privacy when he saw the rear end of the car. He approached the vehicle, saw the shattered windshield and the blood, then the body, and he panicked... at least that's what he said, and there was no reason to disbelieve him. He went back to his car and tried to call it in, but there was no cell reception, so he left the scene and drove until he could make the call. That's why there was a delay of, well, probably just a few minutes."

"You don't think he had anything to do with it?" I already knew the answer, but I had to ask.

"No. He was cleared almost immediately. He was an accountant. We checked his alibi. It was solid. He left work at seven-forty-five. It's no more than a thirty-minute drive from Cleveland to the crime scene, so the timeline fits."

"Any idea how long the body had been there?" I asked.

"The ME put the time of death between six and eight o'clock, so no more than a couple of hours. God only knows how long he would have been there if Hartwell hadn't decided to... relieve himself."

"How about forensics? Anything helpful?"

"They recovered a nine-millimeter bullet from the door-frame, pretty much deformed, not much use, but you never know. The autopsy showed he had some alcohol in his system, just enough to be legally drunk."

"That's it then?" I asked. "No hairs, fibers, fingerprints?"

"Nope... well, plenty of prints, and hairs, but they were all accounted for. Other than that, nothing."

"Sheriff, did you have any thoughts as to what might have happened to Mr. Berryman?"

"Yeah. I think he had a few drinks, met up with the wrong guy... maybe for sex, or maybe he was giving the guy a ride home, and something went wrong. A robbery that went sideways. Simple as that. All of his cash was gone, but we found his wallet outside the car. His credit cards, ID, and photos were all still present. We figured someone wanted to make a quick score, and Berryman didn't want to part with his cash. He paid with his life. Pitiful."

I thanked Sheriff Cane for his help and disconnected the call, then sat back in my chair to think.

So now I had three murders. That meant I did indeed have a serial killer on my hands. I sighed. I felt like crap. I was bone-tired, my shoulders ached, my neck was stiff, and I wanted to go home and drown myself in red wine, but I didn't. I forced myself to call Sheriff Pete McGraw of Huntsville, Alabama.

He was a man of few words, but we talked for maybe ten minutes. He gave me the facts and, in just those few minutes, I learned that William Leeds died in May 2017 as a result of two gunshot wounds to the head, left temple and blah, blah, blah. This time, however, there was a witness who saw Leeds leave a bar with a man smaller and thinner than him with short blond hair.

Yes, I now had victim number four, and by the time I got off the phone, I also had a splitting headache.

It was just after eight o'clock that evening when Ann and Miller came into my office. They both looked like they'd been ridden hard and put away wet. Janet had arrived a few minutes earlier just as perky as ever. *Oh, to be that young and energetic,* I thought, sighing to myself.

I wanted to hear what they all had to say, and I wanted to tell them what we were dealing with, but my heart wasn't in it. I was tired and wanted to get out of there. I needed a long hot bath and a bottle of red... and a pizza.

"What the hell happened to you two?" Janet asked, looking at Ann and Miller. "You look like I felt after last year's Christmas party."

"I only wish we had that much fun," Miller said.

I don't think I ever saw him drink anything harder than a Coke, but that didn't change the fact they both looked exhausted. Miller had dark circles under his eyes, and Ann's eye shadow was smudged from rubbing her eyes. It was a look that, as crazy as this might sound, made her look... sultry.

"We covered almost every bar and hole-in-the-wall in the northeast quarter," Ann said. "There are about five left on our list that we didn't get to."

"Can it wait until tomorrow?" I asked hopefully. "I don't know about you, but my body clock's all out of whack. I need to get back on track, and I'm sure you do too."

"Sure," Ann said, sounding more than a little grateful. "It can wait."

"Okay. Go on home, all of you. Get some rest. We'll get to it tomorrow morning."

11

It was eight-thirty when I arrived home that night. The first thing I did was wrench open the refrigerator door and grab the last of the summer wine, a third of a bottle of Cabernet. I poured the lot into a half-pint glass, flopped down on the couch, cradled the glass in both hands, closed my eyes and sipped, and sipped and sipped until the damn glass was empty. Then I got up, opened a new bottle, poured another half glass, and headed to the bedroom. There I stripped completely, went into the bathroom and took a long hot shower, glass in hand, ducking my head in and out of the water every now and then for a sip.

I toweled myself off, washed the glass in the bathroom sink, returned it to the kitchen, and grabbed the last two slices of a two-day-old pizza from the refrigerator and ate it in... I dunno, three, maybe four bites. Nah, it was more like six, but it was cold, and it was good, and it filled the gap. I looked next at the wine bottle, was tempted, but told myself no, and went to the bedroom where I crawled under the covers, naked as a jaybird. I stretched out between the cold sheets, luxuriating in the feeling of total relaxation. I closed my eyes, a contented smile on my lips, but sleep didn't come easily.

When it did finally come, after what seemed like hours of tossing and turning, it wasn't the deep sleep I craved, but more a sort of balance between sleep and wakefulness.

I was thinking quick, disjointed thoughts that jumped from one victim to the next, leading me around and around until I felt dizzy and nauseous. Cynthia Logan was still a suspect in her husband's death, but her involvement in the other cases was melting away. Actually, it was melting away in Logan's case, too, but I felt I had to hold on to the idea that at least in this case, my case in Chattanooga, she might be the perp. If she did it, or paid someone else to do it, I could close the case and consign the file to the warehouse where it belonged, and Cappy T. Mallard could go back to the morgue.

No, that really wasn't an option. I was already in too deep. And so, eventually, I drifted off into a troubled sleep to dream dreams of shadowy figures in bars and the backs of cars, until finally I woke at six-thirty to the strains of "Don't Worry Be Happy" blasting out from the iPhone at my bedside.

Damn it, I really must change that alarm ringtone.

My head was aching slightly, but it was nothing a couple cups of coffee and two aspirin couldn't cure.

I lay on my back for a few more minutes, breathing deeply, trying to gather my wits. Then I gave up and headed to the kitchen, and then the bathroom, and then stood under a hot shower while my coffee brewed in the kitchen.

I rinsed the shampoo out of my hair, took a deep breath,

and turned the water to cold. It hit my body like a bolt of lightning, took my breath away, made my eyes bug. *Now* I was awake.

I dried off, got dressed—jeans and a pale blue blouse—tied my hair up in a ponytail, filled my to-go mug with hot coffee, and sat down at my computer and took a few minutes to answer some of my work emails. At seven-thirty I refilled my to-go mug and left for work, wondering what the day might have in store for me, and knowing that I had to bring the Chief into the loop and tell him that there was a serial killer on the loose somewhere in the city.

12

"**I**s the Chief in yet?" I asked the duty sergeant as I walked in through the rear entrance to the department. It was just after eight o'clock and raining outside like it was the end of days.

"Isn't he always?" the man said with a curt nod.

I made my way along the hall to the Chief's suite of offices, stood for a moment at the outer door, took a deep breath, knocked, and then entered the outer office where Cathy, his PA, was already at her desk.

"Captain Gazzara," she said with a smile. "You're early. He only arrived a few minutes ago. You know how he is. Could you come back in say... an hour? Give him a chance to compose himself?"

That was a laugh. I'd never known the Chief when he was anything but composed.

"That's not an option, I'm afraid, Cathy. He won't want to be kept waiting for what I have to tell him. D'you mind?"

She tilted her head, frowned slightly, but picked up the phone.

"Captain Gazzara is here. She says it's important."

I heard him growl something. She looked up at me, raised her eyebrows, then said, "Yes, sir," and hung up.

"Take a seat, Captain. He'll be with you shortly."

Shortly was exactly fifteen minutes, and by the time Cathy's phone buzzed and she picked up, I was a nervous wreck.

"You can go in now, Captain." And I did.

Chief Wesley Johnston was seated behind his desk, reading what appeared to be a report, and he was indeed composed: he had a scowl on his face that made him look even more like Hulk Hogan than Hogan did. My heart sank. I'd been hoping he was in a good mood; he wasn't.

"Sit down, Catherine," he said, without looking up.

I sat on a hard seat in front of his desk.

"Chief—" I began, but he held up his hand, his eyes still not rising from the report. He continued to read for several more seconds, seconds during which I grew more and more agitated. Then finally:

"So," he said, looking up and placing the report carefully and deliberately to one side. "What is so important that it can't wait for a more civilized time of the morning?"

I took a deep breath and dived right in. For almost fifteen minutes he listened to me, without saying a word, as I took him through the events of the past three days until finally, I ran out of breath and things to say, so I shut up and waited for him to speak.

He'd been leaning forward as he listened to my diatribe, his elbows on his desktop, eyes narrowed, concentrating. The man never took notes. I figured he must have some sort of eidetic memory.

When I finished speaking, he leaned back in his chair and stared at me.

"How many people know about all this?" he asked quietly.

"About Logan? Just my team. About the victim Mallard, just me. About Berryman and Leeds... me and the two Sheriffs. That's it, so far. I'll bring my team up to speed when I go to my office."

He thought for a moment, then shook his head slightly and said, "What leads do you have, Kate?"

I looked down at my knees, then back up at him and said, "None... Well, I was thinking the ex-wife, but I'm beginning to think that's one hell of a stretch. I'll follow it up of course, but... Other than that, none."

"You have to keep this under wraps, Kate. No, I'm not suggesting a cover-up, but we have to keep it out of the hands of the press until... We can't have this go public, not yet. When we do it, we do it together. In the meantime, keep the circle as small as possible: just your team and Mike Willis, and tell them to be extra careful in their inquiries. They are not to mention the word 'serial' ever, understood?"

I nodded, and I did understand. Ours is a small city, and the idea that there was a psycho killer at large, well, it was disconcerting, to say the least.

"I trust you, Catherine, but I want you to keep me informed every step of the way."

I nodded.

He said, "Go do your thing, Captain."

I stood, opened my mouth to speak, thought better of it, nodded, and left him to his thoughts; my own were spinning almost out of control.

13

From the Chief's office I went straight to the incident room. My intent was to gather my troops and spend the next hour planning strategy, but as I exited the elevator, I heard someone shouting.

"You don't know what you're talking about!"

Then I heard Ann's voice. "Mr. Brown, you need to calm down!"

Ann was sitting at her desk, talking to a small man who looked to be about thirty years old. It was him who was doing the shouting, at her. He was wearing one of those camouflage hats with the panels that hang down the back like he might suddenly be transported to the desert and need his neck protected from the sun, a red and black flannel shirt over a T-shirt and baggy jeans, with a heavy camouflage jacket on top of that. The laces of his boots were untied and, as he talked, he slipped his left foot in and out of its shoe. A nervous tick of sorts?

"I am calm! This is calm! Believe me! You'd be sorry if I wasn't calm!"

What the hell?

"Sir, if you don't calm down," Ann said quietly, as Janet and Miller, both at their desks, looked on smiling, "I'll have you tossed in the tank until you do. Now, take it easy and tell me what happened slowly, so we can get you the help you need." Ann pinched her lips together and waited for him to speak.

I went to Miller's desk and stood by, watching.

"I told you. All right?" he said, somewhat mollified. "I was assaulted."

"From the beginning, please?" Ann didn't look up from her notes.

"I was on my way home last night, from Mickey's tavern. There was a girl I used to know. She was waiting for me in the alley by my apartment. She and her sister came out of nowhere." He looked around. By then everyone in the room was watching and listening. "I know what you're all thinking, but I was raised that you don't hit a girl."

Janet shrugged.

Miller nodded in agreement. "That's how I was raised too," he concurred and was gifted with an enthusiastic nod from the man.

"Yeah, well, she jumped out of the alley and slapped me," he said, then waited for the collective gasp he thought he deserved but didn't get. "And two weeks ago she vandalized my car."

"Did you file a police report?" Ann asked.

"No. But I know she did it. She knows my car. She told me she'd get me back. It's a red Bronco."

"Everyone knows my car, too, Mr. Brown, a red Monte Carlo," Ann said sarcastically. "Sometimes it gets dinged, scratched, dented, a tire goes flat. It happens. Okay, okay, I hear you," she said as he opened his mouth to protest. "How long have you been with this... girl?"

"We've been on-again, off-again for about six months," he said with a shrug.

"Had you been drinking?" Ann asked.

"I had two beers," he replied.

I smiled. They all only have two beers, don't they? The guy arrested for plowing into a car full of nuns only had two beers. The woman who drove her car onto a railroad track also had only two beers. The guy that drove through the drug store window only had two beers.

"What about your girlfriend? Had she—"

"Ex! My ex-girlfriend!" He sat back on the steel chair and spread his legs wide, slouching, his hands in his jacket pockets.

"Had she been drinking?" Ann asked loudly.

"Probably," he snapped.

"But you don't know for sure," Ann replied.

"No, I don't know. I wasn't with her, was I?"

"What's her name?" Ann asked, then said, "Look, Mr. Brown, are you sure you want to do this? Do you really want your ex-girlfriend hauled in here in handcuffs and processed?"

Brown chewed his thumbnail, thinking, then said, "Can I think for a minute?"

"Take all the time you need, Mr. Brown. Do you mind if I talk with my captain while you're thinking?" Ann said, pointing to me.

He turned in his seat to look at me. He was wearing glasses, big glasses that gave him an owl-like look. His face was thin and pale. He turned back to Ann and shrugged. She stood and joined me at Miller's desk.

"You need to get rid of him ASAP," I said. "We have real work to do. Where the hell did he come from?"

"He walked in through the front door about thirty minutes ago," she said. "He said he wanted to file an assault complaint. I happened to catch it, sorry."

I shook my head. It happened more often than you'd think.

"What's the plan?" Janet asked.

"I need everyone in my office. Where's Hawk? Anybody know?"

"He went to get coffee," Janet said.

"Okay," I said, "Ann wrap that thing up and let's get to it. My office in fifteen minutes, everyone."

"You got it, Cap," Ann said, turning to go back to her desk. "Hey, where'd he go?" The man was nowhere to be seen.

"Obviously had a change of heart," I said, and I left them to it.

Ten minutes later they all trooped into my office and took seats around the table, Miller to my left, Janet to my right, Robar and Hawk opposite.

Miller opened his laptop, connected it to a small projector, and before I could stop him began tapping away on the keys.

"Hold on, Lennie," I said and looked at them each in turn. "There have been some developments... a lot of developments. It appears that we're dealing with a serial killer."

I swear, you could have cut the silence with a knife.

14

"You gotta be shittin' me," Hawk growled. "How the hell did you come up with that idea?"

"We now have a total of four victims, that I know of," I said, standing and stepping over to the board.

"Jack Logan," I said. "Cappy T. Mallard." I wrote the name at the top of the board, added the date, 2013, and taped up the five photographs from the murder book.

"Lawrence Berryman, Dalton, Georgia, 2015," I said, adding his name and the date of his demise to the board. "And William Leeds, Huntsville, Alabama, 2017." I added his details to the board and then sat down again. "And there may be more, many more."

I looked at the board, then at my team.

"All four were killed over a period of five years and found in exactly the same way, our friend Logan being the latest, with Cappy Miller, the first, that I know of. Comments?"

And they came in a deluge. It took more than an hour for me to relate my findings. Through it all, Hawk sat stoically across the table from me and said barely a word. The result, in the end, was a confounded silence all round with everyone staring up at the board, still horribly bare.

Finally, Hawk said, "Okay, I believe you. There are too many coincidences for it not to be true, but we need more information. When are we getting the goods on Berryman and Leeds?"

Talk about coincidence; just as he said it there was a knock at my door. I called for the knocker to come in, and a uniformed officer stepped inside.

"From Sheriff Cane," he said, dumping a sealed banker's box on my desk. "One of his deputies just dropped it off, said it was urgent. He's waiting downstairs, needs a signature." He handed me a form. I scanned through the list of the box's contents, and signed the form, tore off my copy, and handed it back: the chain of evidence was complete. No, I didn't check the contents of the box; that would've taken too long. I took the list at face value and signed: not the best practice, but you have to exercise a little trust now and again, and this was one of those times.

I thanked the uniform and he nodded and left, closing the door behind him.

"Looks like we already have Berryman," I said, opening the envelope taped to the top of the box and reading aloud the note inside. "I thought I'd send it on, rather than have you wait for FedEx. Let me know if you need help. Best, and good luck. Cane." *Nice of him to rush it. Not solving this one must have bothered him.*

"How's that for service?" I said, unsealing the box and opening it.

Together, we searched through Berryman's files, reports,

trace evidence, and found little more than we already had. There were, though, several sealed evidence bags inside the box. One contained Berryman's wallet, another several strands of blond hair, and another contained a badly damaged, full metal jacket nine-millimeter bullet. Cane had been right when he said there wasn't much evidence, but as he also said, you never know what might help.

I set all of the evidence bags aside for transfer to Mike Willis, and together the five of us concentrated on the reports and photographs.

By the time we'd finished, it was almost noon, and the big board was beginning to look like we had the germ of a plan; funny how looks can be so deceiving.

It was at that point that I noticed Miller was growing more agitated almost by the minute.

"Hey, what's wrong with you?" I asked.

"I... I've been running security footage, where there was any, and I found something, I think."

"Why the hell didn't you say something earlier, Lennie?" I asked. "Damn, we need direction and if you found something... Okay, come on, spill it."

"If you'll just give me a minute... while I..." He tapped on the keys of the laptop, the projector lit up, and, "Here we go," he said. "This is footage from one of the bars Ann and I visited."

I watched as the wall behind Hawk and Ann lit up with moving images as Miller pulled up the grainy black and white video.

"Geez," Janet griped. "Is that the best we can do? We can put a man on the moon but we can't get half-way decent footage on our security cameras. Look at that. It's crap!"

Miller, feeling the need to defend modern technology, tried to explain why the footage from such places was almost always poor.

"Do you have any idea the damage that cigarette smoke does to the camera lenses, or any other kind of electrical devices?" he asked. "The only time fresh air gets into a bar is when the doors are open, which is only when someone goes in or out; the rest of the time the air is like pudding. There's moisture, dust, dirt, grime, *smoke*, and grease if there's a kitchen, and yes, most of them do provide food in one form or another. The lens ends up with a thick film of grease on it, thus the deterioration of the image. It's not like the pristine conditions we have in our homes where—"

"Miller, have you ever kissed a girl?" Janet teased.

"Does family count?" he replied innocently, making me choke back a chuckle. Ann was not so discreet and laughed loudly.

"All right," I said, "that's enough. Just tell us what we're looking at, Lennie."

"This is from the bar Second Base," Miller said. "You remember it, right, Ann? That place where—"

"Yeah, I remember," Ann said, interrupting his flow.

"Cute name," Janet replied.

"Yes, well, Mr. Logan will show up in a minute. It's just a small sports bar. There's nothing fancy about it. Nothing special about the crowd. But look, here we go," he said as Ann went to stand behind him, her arms folded.

I watched intently and, after a minute or so I saw a man enter and take a seat at the bar.

"That's him," Miller said. "See, look at the photos. It's him, Jack Logan." And it was.

Logan had sat down. Then he looked along the bar to his left and saw something that seemed to upset him, because he stood up again, turned away, and walked quickly out of the bar. Lennie stopped the projector. The final image of Logan walking to the door still on the screen. It was time-stamped four-oh-nine, roughly an hour before the opening of the ninety-minute window during which he died.

"Well, that's weird," I said. "Did you interview the bartender?"

"Yeah," Miller replied. "I went down there this morning. He was cleaning up. He remembered Logan coming in and then leaving right away when he saw a woman at the far end of the bar. She's a regular, and she'd had an altercation with Logan several weeks earlier. He said her name was Cynthia. He didn't know her last name."

My eyebrows shot up, my mouth hung open, and I was sure my heart stopped for a brief second.

"Shit! Seriously? Is she on the video? When did she leave? Did she go after him?"

I prayed for Miller to tell me yes, but he just shook his head and said, "The bartender said she didn't leave until after last call; that was at one o'clock in the morning."

"Did she make any calls?" I asked. "Did anyone follow him out?"

"No, she didn't, and she was just about legless when she left. I can run the footage, but there's nothing more to see. No one left the bar until almost forty minutes after Logan did.

"Looks like Cynthia Logan has an alibi," Ann said.

"Unless she paid someone to do it for her," Janet said.

"So what's the next step?" Ann asked as she walked back around the table and sat down.

I thought for a minute, then said, "Ann, you and Miller go check out the remaining bars on your list. He went somewhere after he left Second Base. We need to find out where.

"Janet, I need you to take those evidence bags down to Mike Willis. And see if he has any news about those hairs, and if he was able to match the bullet Hawk found. Also, Miller, before you and Ann head out, I need Cynthia Logan's phone records. Jack Logan's too... Good work, Lennie."

He grinned, nodded, and said, "Thanks, Cap. Check your printer. I sent both sets of records to you before we started our meeting. I thought you'd probably need them so—"

"Well done, Lennie. I appreciate it. Now, both of you get out of here. Go find out where Logan ate his last meal. It has to be somewhere close to Second Base."

And they left.

I spent the next fifteen minutes or so talking to Hawk about the Cappy Mallard case, my idea being that he could begin following up with the witnesses, especially the lead detective, a Sergeant Paul Hicks, now retired.

I was about to send him on his way when I heard footsteps in the hall outside my office. A few seconds later, my door burst open and Ann Robar charged in, followed by Miller.

"You're not going to believe this," she snarled. "Some son of a bitch has slashed my freakin' tires!"

15

We pulled the security footage from the cameras in front of the building, and none of us were surprised to see the enigmatic Mr. Brown—Ann had somehow neglected to get his first name—walk calmly around Ann's car and slash all four tires. *Boy, she must have really pissed him off,* I thought. *How did he know it was her car?*

Ann called for a wrecker to come get her car, and then the motor pool for an unmarked cruiser. She put out a BOLO for Brown, and the two of them left again to go finish their canvassing.

By the time I was done that day, it was already dark outside and I was starving. We'd missed lunch, and I hadn't eaten a thing other than the sausage and egg sandwich earlier that morning.

I stopped off at Publix on the way home and bought a

whole rotisserie chicken and two bottles of a halfway decent Cabernet, and by decent, I mean they had corks instead of screw caps.

It was almost seven o'clock when I parked my car in my spot outside my apartment. I was beat, so I just sat there for a minute with my eyes closed, thankful that the long day was over.

Finally, I took a deep breath, shoved open the car door, grabbed my groceries, and headed to the front door, wondering how many other folks were about to settle down for the night with a whole chicken and two bottles of wine.

For a minute, and only for a minute, I felt guilty. My body was going to suffer for what I was about to do, but I didn't care. All I wanted to do was eat and sleep... and drink a little.

As I approached the steps to my apartment, I was greeted by a neighbor and his dog. He was talking to a woman I didn't know but assumed must be another of my neighbors from the adjoining block. I'd chatted with the guy a couple of times before about the weather and work and such. He was in construction if I remembered right. He was just a nice guy who liked to watch sports and drink a few beers.

The woman was petite. Her hair short and blond and she was wearing jeans and a short black leather jacket over what looked like a tank top.

"How are they treating you down at the station, Detective?" he asked.

"Can't complain. And if I did, no one would listen," I said, smiling as I walked past them and on up the steps.

"She's a detective, can you believe that?" my neighbor said to his friend.

"She's pretty," I heard the woman say.

For a moment, I felt a little better about myself. I guess after a day like I'd just endured, a little normalcy put things back into perspective.

I tended to forget that sometimes, no matter what crap I have to deal with on a daily basis, the rest of the world keeps right on turning. *Don't it just, though?*

I closed the door to my apartment, and on the rest of the frickin' world, dumped my chicken on the kitchen counter, opened one of the bottles, poured myself a half a glass, and said, "Alexa, play some mariachi music."

Yeah, that's what I said, mariachi. I don't know why. Maybe it's the cheerfulness of it, but mariachi always does it for me.

I added some ice to my glass of Cabernet, tore a leg off the chicken, and all but fell into my recliner and then tried to let go. It wasn't easy, but I forced myself to listen to the trumpets and not to think about work.

As I sat there, glass in hand, my eyes closed, listening to the music of Mexico, I suddenly realized I hadn't had any time off in almost two years. I needed a vacation. I had time coming to me. Maybe I'd go someplace cold. Colorado maybe. I'd never been skiing. Maybe I'd meet someone to snuggle under a blanket with and sip hot cider, with a little rum in it, of course.

Nah, I need hot sunshine, a bikini, turquoise waters, and calypso music. I wonder if Harry could put in a word for me at Calypso Key... Shit! Where the hell did that come from?

Calypso Key was where Harry married Amanda. That

was the last place I needed to go. *Ah, forget it. Who needs a vacation anyway?*

Finally, as my eyelids grew heavy, I struggled out of the recliner, pulled the curtains closed, stashed the rest of the chicken in the fridge, poured myself another half glass of wine, and went to bed.

In the darkness, I turned off my phone—something I rarely ever did—stripped off my clothes, climbed into bed naked, took a last sip of wine, lay back on the pillows, closed my eyes and was soon lost among the white-topped mountains, log cabins, snowflakes and hot chocolate. And, for the first time in weeks, I slept well. I didn't wake until the alarm went off at six-thirty the following morning.

16

The next morning was Friday the thirteenth. Now, I'm not usually superstitious about such things, but that one started with a bang, literally. And from that point on, events began to move very quickly and all downhill.

It was just after eight-thirty when I walked into the incident room that morning to find most of my team already there, primed and ready to go. I'd stopped along the way to get my usual breakfast sandwich and a fill-up of my metal coffee tumbler. After the best night's sleep in many a long day, I was feeling pretty chipper.

"Hey guys," I said brightly. "How y'all is this rainy Friday morning?"

I was answered by a chorus of good mornings and smart remarks, and I smiled and thought that life was good, probably better than I deserved.

"My car should be ready later this morning," Ann said, her voice was cheery or at least as cheery as Detective Ann Robar ever got.

"How about I run you over to get it?" Miller said, suggestively, giving her a playful nudge.

She smiled, shook her head, and said, "Not today, sonny." And Miller looked suitably chastened.

"I... I didn't mean—"

"I know you didn't, sweetie," Ann said. "Of course you can take me."

"Where's Janet?" Hawk asked. "It's not like her to be late."

I looked around at her cubicle. Her computer wasn't on. Her notebooks hadn't been disturbed, and her chair was still tucked neatly beneath her desk. I took out my phone and called her. She didn't answer.

"She probably stopped somewhere to get coffee," I said. "Give her a few more minutes; she'll be here."

I stood there talking to them about the case for several more minutes, ending with a repetition of my warning that Chief Johnston wanted everything kept under wraps for as long as possible. Then I turned to go into my office, and my phone buzzed in my jacket pocket. I barely heard it, and I certainly didn't feel it. *Damn, I forgot to turn the ringer back on... Un-for-frickin' believable.*

"Gazzara," I answered, and then my world turned upside down; Friday the thirteenth had begun in earnest.

"Captain," the receptionist said. "I'm sorry to call you on your cell, but you're not in your office. I have a Doctor Joon Napai on the phone. She insists on talking to you; says it's an emergency."

"Put her through, please."

"Captain Gazzara?"

"Yes, doctor. What can I do for you?"

"I tried calling you last night, Captain, and again this morning. I even left messages. Your Sergeant Janet Toliver was brought into the hospital last night—"

"What?" I asked, stunned, interrupting her. My mouth had gone completely dry.

"She's conscious, and talking, and she insisted I call you to let you know. I'll go now—"

"Wait, what happened to her? How is she?"

"According to her boyfriend—he's here with her—she was assaulted and beaten. She received a very nasty crack on the back of the head, and she has a hairline fracture of the skull that should heal quite quickly. She also has some superficial facial trauma that will also heal nicely. Her two broken ribs, though; they will take a while to heal. Now, I have to go. She's in room 2007. Please feel free to visit." And with that, she hung up, leaving me standing there in a stupor. I just couldn't believe it. Janet wasn't a careless person, nor was she easily fooled.

What the hell could have happened?

"Cap? Is everything all right?" Hawk asked.

I know I told them what had happened and I remember the looks of shock and worry on their faces, but for the life of me, I can't recall exactly what I said.

"I'll go with you to the hospital," Ann said.

"No. I want you and Miller to finish canvassing the bars. Go shake some trees and see what falls. Somebody somewhere must have seen something.

"Hawk, I need your help. I need you to study the files and put together a map. I've been looking at it by myself way too long, and I'm going cross-eyed. I need a fresh pair of eyes on it, yours. By the time I get back, I want something we can work with and a full breakdown of all four cases, including Huntsville and Dalton. FedEx should deliver Huntsville before ten, any minute in fact. Go to it, people."

Without another word, I walked out of the building and drove to the Erlanger Hospital Emergency room. I barely remember the ride over there. My mind was in a whirl. I parked in the lot opposite the emergency room, half-ran inside, flashed my badge and asked where I'd find room 2007.

A kind-faced, elderly gentleman sporting a volunteer's badge that proclaimed his name was Bill led me through a set of double doors, down a long corridor until:

"Here you go, Detective," Bill said. "Let us know if you need anything." He smiled and his brown eyes twinkled. As much as I didn't feel like it, I couldn't help but smile back.

"Anybody home?" I asked quietly as I pulled the curtain aside and stuck my head through.

Janet was in the bed, with her boyfriend sitting next to her, holding her hand. She looked... awful. Her left eye was swollen shut and her top lip, puffy and purple, looked... well, she had a fat lip, and that described it perfectly. Her chest was heavily bandaged, and she looked like hell.

"It's part of the job, right Detective?" The boyfriend smiled sadly as he rose to his feet. "At least, that's what she tells me." He looked fondly down at her, then back at me, offered me his hand and said, "I'm Adam. You're Detective Gazzara, right?"

He was a big bull of a guy, did something in construction, as I recalled.

"You can call me—" I began.

But before I could complete the thought, Janet opened

her eyes and interrupted me, "Hey, Kate," she muttered and tried to smile, but all she managed was to wince with pain.

"What the hell, Toliver?" I said, patting Adam's arm and stepping to her side. "Look, if you wanted time off, all you had to do was ask, okay? Can you talk? Can you tell me what happened?"

She nodded slightly, winced, then said, "Yeah, but I don't know what happened. Adam and me, we'd arranged to meet outside that bar, you know, Second Base where Logan was last seen. I arrived first, but instead of waiting for him, I decided to go take a quick look. I parked curbside and was just getting out of my car when there's this tremendous blow to the back of my head and... and then I'm on the ground. My head's spinning, I can't see anything, and then I get kicked in the face. Next thing, someone is kicking the crap out of me, see?" She tried to look down at her bandaged ribs, but couldn't. "And that's all I know," she said.

I turned to her boyfriend and said, "Did you see what happened, Adam?"

"Like she said, we were supposed to meet outside the bar. When I got there, I see her car but she's not in it, not so far as I could see. So I step up and look inside... nothing. Then I hear a moan, like, so I go around the car and I find her lying on her back, on the ground, in the street next to the car, bleeding from her face."

"Did you get a look at the guy who did this to you, Janet?" I asked.

"No. I went down like a sack of potatoes. But I think I got a glimpse of his girlfriend. I saw a tattoo on the back of her hand when the bitch reached for my purse. But my head was spinning, and everything was wavy and out of focus." She looked at Adam, who was, I could tell, holding back tears.

"I'll be right back," he said and slipped quietly out of the room. And that seemed like a good time for me to go talk to the doctor.

Doctor Joon Napai was just a little thing, no taller than Janet. She had smooth skin, and I figured she must be somewhere in her forties, but gray strands were already present among her jet-black hair. Her job in the Emergency Room probably took its toll on her, like mine was doing to me. She informed me that she would be keeping Janet in the hospital, probably for several days—standard procedure for anyone with a serious head injury—to make sure she didn't have a concussion and to make sure she'd give herself the time needed for her ribs to mend. For that I was grateful, because knowing Janet as I did, she'd be back at work as soon as she could stand up.

I returned to Janet's room and had a few words with Adam, who assured me he intended to stay with her. For that I was also thankful. I asked him to give me a few minutes alone with her, and he nodded and said he'd go get a bite to eat.

"You still feel like talking?" I asked.

"Absolutely," she said, wincing.

I shook my head, then said, "Will he be okay, Adam?" I asked.

"Yeah, he'll get over it," she said. "This is the first time I've gotten hurt... I tell you what, Kate. These are some fiiiine pain-killers."

"I'll bet they are." I smiled.

"So, you think there were two of them, then?"

"I guess."

"You said the woman reached for your purse?"

"Yes, she took my cash, all of it. I had almost three hundred in my wallet. Damn it."

"That's all they took, just your cash?"

"Yes, just the cash."

"Not your credit cards?"

"Nope."

"Tell me about the tattoo."

"It was kinda blue... and swirly..." She shook her head, then said, "I'm sorry. That's all I can remember."

"Interesting," I muttered, more to myself than to Janet.

17

"**H**ey Cap, I need to show you something," Hawk said when I walked into the situation room. "How's Janet, by the way?"

That's Hawk for you. He knew she was alive, so that was good enough; she'd get over it.

"She's banged up quite a bit," I said. "But she's doing okay. I'll fill you in later. What d'you have for me?"

I was happy for the distraction, but more than a little bothered by the odds that two people, two police officers, both members of my team, Ann and Janet, had been targeted within forty-eight hours. It was too much of a coincidence.

"Sheriff Cane's people in Dalton recovered a badly damaged bullet from the victim's car door frame," he said. "And, as you know, I recovered another from the barn on Route 18..." He paused, stared at me, a sloppy grin on his face.

"So?" I said impatiently.

"Mike Willis made the match," he said triumphantly. "They were both fired from the same gun."

Try as I might, I couldn't feel as excited about it as he obviously was. So they matched? So what? I'd already figured they would. Big deal. It didn't help the investigation. In fact, it complicated it—confirmed that we did indeed have a predator on our hands.

"That's good, right?" he said. "But there's more. McGraw's ME took one out of Leeds' head. It also matches."

And there it was, confirmation. We were now officially dealing with a serial killer. Whoop-de-doo.

"Come on, Kate," he said. "This is big."

"Okay, Hawk. I agree. It's good to know. Now, all we have to do is find the gun and we have our killer. Any ideas how we might do that?" I didn't mean to be so bitchy to him, but I was frustrated and upset about what had happened to Janet, and even more upset that I was now dealing with something that could quickly get out of hand. Oh yes, I was worried the press might get hold of it.

I put my hands on my hips and waited, not really expecting him to give me an answer, but of course he did.

"Well, according to what we know, the perp has been using the same weapon for more than five years," Hawk said. "I doubt he's going to toss it in the river and go find a new one now. These people are creatures of habit. They also believe they're invincible."

"Did you see anything in the case files that could give us a lead on where they might strike next?" I asked. "Our victims are all overweight, middle-aged men. Some are single. Some are married."

"There isn't a sexual component involved," Hawk replied. "As far as I can tell, it's all about the money."

"That's bizarre," I said. "We've got a maniac prowling the bars and killing for a few dollars. None of them had more than two or three hundred bucks on them, right? Sure, people have died for less, but I get the feeling there's more to our subject's motivation—"

"Kate." I heard my name and whirled around to see Chief Johnston approaching. I'd been hoping I'd be able to skate through the day without having to talk to him.

"Hey, Chief. I was just going to call you," I said, lying through my teeth. "We're making progress, not much, but some. Willis has been able to establish that the bullet Hawkins recovered from the Logan scene matches three other cold cases—"

"That's all very interesting," he said, "but that's not what I want to talk to you about. Your office, Captain, I think. Now!"

What the hell? I wondered.

We sat down together at the table. He put his elbows on the tabletop, clasped his hands together in front of him, stared at me over them, and began, "You remember when I asked you if you had anything you wanted to tell me, so I wouldn't be surprised if I heard from Internal Affairs?" His eyes bore into me.

"Yes, I remember. So?"

My heart skipped a beat as I waited for him to explain.

"Captain Volker called me about an hour ago."

Volker ran the IA department. My heart skipped another beat.

"A Mr. Alvin Brown called him and said that he came

in yesterday morning to file a complaint against his girl-friend, and during his interview, you made an inappropriate suggestion to him. What the hell did you say to him, Kate?"

I couldn't help but grin. In fact, I almost laughed out loud.

"What's so funny, Captain?"

"That man's a nut case," I said. "First, it was Ann Robar that conducted that interview, not me. I just happened to stop by while he was yelling at her. Second, she asked him to think about if he wanted to go through with what he was doing while she talked to me for a minute and, while we talked, the idiot disappeared. Third, he went straight out of the building and slashed all four of Ann's tires; we have him on surveillance footage doing it. I made an inappropriate suggestion? Seriously? Ann's about to have him arrested, if she can find him. Maybe she'll get lucky, now that we know his full name." I stopped talking. I could see by his face I'd said enough.

"I thought it sounded a little off-the-wall, Kate," John-ston said. "If he'd claimed you'd slapped him, I might have tended to believe him, but sexual harassment? No. Forget it. I'll handle Volker. So, now that we have that out of the way, what's the situation with the Logan case?"

"There's something going on, Chief, something I can't quite get a handle on. This guy slashed Ann's tires. The same guy files a complaint against me, and Janet got beaten half to death outside the bar where our victim Logan was last seen. It's all a little coincidental, don't you think?"

I folded my hands and leaned forward. "I have a bad feeling about Brown. We need to find him, and quickly. I'd hate for something to happen to Miller or Hawk or both before we can grab him, if it is him."

"I agree," he said. "How's Toliver doing? She'll recover fully, I presume?" The corner of his left eye began to twitch; something I'd never seen before.

"She's at Erlanger," I replied. "She has two broken ribs and a fractured skull. It's not quite as bad as it sounds. It's just a hairline fracture, but still, they're keeping her for a few more days, worried about a possible concussion. She should be able to go home next week, if all goes well. Her boyfriend, Adam, is staying with her."

"There's no security footage of the attack, I assume?" he asked.

"Unfortunately, no."

"So, we don't know if it was Brown... Better get a uniform over there, just in case. I'll go see her this afternoon. She is allowed visitors, correct?"

I nodded, thinking about what he'd just said. *Could it possibly be Brown we're looking for?*

"And you," Johnston said. "Do I need to assign a uniform to follow you around, too?"

"Are you serious, Chief?" It was a stupid question, because I could see from the look on his face that he was.

"No, Chief," I said. "You don't need to worry about me. I'll be doing things by the book. I promise." I don't know why I said I promise. I knew damn well it was a promise I couldn't keep, and that he didn't believe me.

"Chief, have you ever known a case like this?" I asked.

He slowly shook his head and said, "What do you think, Kate? Of course not, but then, I was never a detective." He stood, looked down at me, and said, "That'll be all for now,

Kate. Get back to work. Catch this guy before he kills again."

I nodded, and he left my office. I picked up my desk phone and called Hawk. Miller and Ann had returned. I asked him to join me and bring them with him.

"Everything okay, Cap?" Ann asked.

"Oh yeah," I lied. "What have you got for me?"

"Yes, I can see that," Ann said sarcastically. "Well, I think I have something that'll make you feel better. We found the place where Logan ate his last meal, a bar and grill called The Sovereign. It's a half-assed sort of establishment: just a long bar, a couple of tables, two big flat-screen TVs, a griddle, and a couple of deep fat fryers. The place is... let's just say, I think a call to the restaurant inspector might be in order."

"And we've got video," Miller said, slipping a thumb drive into his laptop. His fingers flew over the keyboard, and instantly, we were watching video footage from inside the bar.

"You can see our victim clearly," Ann said, pointing at the screen. "This is him sitting at the bar, alone, drinking a beer and eating a burger. He doesn't look intoxicated to me."

I said nothing. I just watched as the scene played out. There were some dozen people in the bar, none of them doing anything out of the ordinary. Most of them were staring up at one or the other of the two TVs on the wall behind the bar. Some patrons were talking to each other, but not a lot; no sound, unfortunately. The footage was time-stamped four-twenty-eight, just nineteen minutes after he'd left Second Base. *He must have driven straight over there,* I thought.

"It looks depressing," I said. "Is this all there is?"

"No, wait, there's more," Ann said. "Here we go: enter our suspect. That's him, there."

A small man walked into the bar and sat down next to Logan. We couldn't see his face; he seemed to be consciously avoiding the camera. He had blond hair, that was obviously in need of a trim, and was wearing a heavy camouflage jacket over what might have been a white T-shirt and jeans. He said something to Logan, then looked at the bartender, then again at Logan, all the time keeping his head down. Logan gestured to the bartender and two beers were placed in front of them.

"Looks like they're getting along fine," I said. "I wish to hell I could see his face. Is that him, Ann? Is it Brown?"

She slowly shook her head, then said, "I dunno. Could be, but this guy isn't wearing glasses. Brown was... And he was wearing that hunter's cap, so I never did see his hair. It's hard to tell... Might be."

We continued to watch as Logan bought the man another drink, stood, slapped him on the shoulder, and moved to leave. The man in the camo jacket turned, stared after him, said something, and Logan returned and stood beside him, and the two became engaged in an animated conversation.

"I think Logan's new friend wants him to stick around," Miller said.

Hawk leaned closer to get a better look at the man then pointed to the screen.

"Look at his hair. It's about the right length and color. We may have a match. What d'you think?"

"Hey, don't touch the screen," Miller said, slapping the back of his hand. "You'll mess it up."

"Yeah, okay, nerd," Hawk said.

"Hey, I'm just saying," Miller snapped back.

"Would you two knuckleheads quiet down," Ann replied. "Leave his shit alone, Hawk. You know how sensitive he is."

"Oh hell, Robar," he said, without looking up from the screen. "I didn't even look in your direction, so as I see it, you don't need to be interjecting yourself into the conversation."

"One of these days, Hawk," Ann said, "someone's going to teach you a lesson," and she bumped him with her hip as she scooted past him.

"Yeah, yeah, so you say," Hawk said, still not looking up. "Cap, I think Logan is wanting to leave, but the little guy is trying to get him to stay. Then look, see? It's the little guy who leaves first, not Logan, he didn't finish his beer and he looks pissed."

"He waited for him, outside," I muttered thoughtfully. "The little bastard ambushed him. You think it could be Brown, Ann?" I asked again.

"I don't know. It could be... If we could just get a look at his face."

"Did you talk to the bartender?"

"We talked to a bartender, but he wasn't on duty that night. He didn't know anything," Ann said. "But the bar owner who provided us with the footage said that the bartender that did work that night was off until this afternoon; his name is Mickey, by the way, the bartender, that is, not the owner."

I looked at my watch. It was almost two-thirty.

"What time do they open?" I asked.

"They're open already, since eleven," Miller said.

"Come on, Ann," I said. "Let's go talk to Mickey. The rest of you stay on it. Keep digging. Lennie, see what you can find out about an Alvin Brown. And I need a screenshot of those two. Can you send it to my printer?" He nodded, and I continued, "Hawk, you check in with Willis. See if he's come up with anything new. We'll be back, okay?"

I grabbed the image from my printer, then my jacket, and we left.

The Sovereign was just as nasty in real life as it was on the video footage. We walked through the front door into a dingy, half-lit world where the air was awash with the smell of stale beer and cigarette smoke. It wasn't quite as bad as the smell of my grandmother's basement after it flooded in 1996, but it was damn close, and I wondered about the people who habitually congregated in such places. Surely there was something better.

The barstools, those that weren't occupied, were old and made of wood with short, stubby backs. The walls were papered with promotional beer posters featuring sports heroes from a bygone era: the Atlanta Braves, the Falcons, and for some reason, some featured players in Green Bay Packer uniforms. There was even one poster featuring the great Spanish bullfighter, El Cordobés, a tribute to the bar's Hispanic clientele, I presumed. There was also a dartboard and a long row of small, framed photographs of people I could only assume were regular customers.

Ann and I took seats at the bar, trying to ignore the attention we—two seemingly single women—had attracted from the moment we walked in, and we waited for the bartender to see us. He was at the far end of the bar, talking to a young woman while washing glasses at the same time.

He was a pleasant-looking guy, despite the burgeoning beer belly. His heavily muscled arms bore an assortment of tattoos, including an American flag crossed with the red flag of the Marines. The words Semper Fi were tattooed in big letters over the flags, and God Bless America beneath.

The bottles on the shelves behind him were nothing special either: cheap bourbon, off-brand scotch, gin I'd never even heard of. It was a place where Absolut was the most expensive vodka and Budweiser came in a can.

He glanced at me, jerked his chin up, and held up a finger, signaling he'd be right with me. I discretely opened my jacket and displayed my badge. He grinned, nodded, and came right over, still wiping out a glass. I showed him my ID.

"D'you mind?" he asked, taking it from me. He held it up to a light over the shelves, nodded, and handed it back to me.

"Was that just to impress me, or was it routine?" I asked.

"Can't be too careful, can we, Captain?" This guy was either a stickler for the rules or he was full of shit; I figured it was probably the latter.

"You Mickey?" I asked.

"Mickey O'Donnell, at your service. What can I do for you two lovely ladies?"

"Cut the crap, Mickey. You were working on Tuesday, so I'm told. Is that right?"

"Yes, ma'am," he said, smiling, obviously unperturbed by my tone.

"Do you remember seeing this man come in here?" I handed him a copy of a photograph of Logan, one his wife had provided.

"Yes. Sure. He came in to watch the ballgame."

"Had you ever seen him in here before?" I asked.

"Once in a while, not often. Loves his football. I felt kinda bad for him though."

"Why is that?" Ann asked.

He shrugged and said, "The guy came in to watch the game, right? But he got himself tangled up with one of my regulars. He made the mistake of buying the guy a beer. After that, the guy just wouldn't leave him alone."

"Do you have a name?" I asked.

"Nate. He goes by Nate."

"Is this him?" I showed Mickey the screenshot taken from The Sovereign's surveillance footage. Mickey nodded and handed the photo back to me.

"Yeah, that's him."

"And you say he's a regular here?" I asked as the front door opened behind me. I turned and looked, hoping I was about to get lucky and Nate would walk right on in. But no such luck. The guy who did walk in was at least six feet tall with a heavily weathered face and Dumbo ears. He sat down at the far corner of the bar, next to the woman the bartender had so recently been talking to, waved at Mickey, and yelled in a high-pitched voice for a Bud.

"Go ahead," I said. "I'm in no hurry."

I looked around, checking out the clientele, and I noticed a woman staring at me. She was by herself, an older lady who looked as worn out as the posters on the walls. She had a cigarette between her fingers and kept flicking it nervously. I had a feeling, from the way she kept looking at me, then down at the cigarette, then back at me again, that she wanted to talk to me.

"Hold the fort for a minute," I said to Ann, then I got up from my stool, walked over to the woman and sat down next to her.

"You're a cop?" she asked. Her voice was scratchy, raspy; she was obviously a heavy smoker.

"Detective Gazzara, Chattanooga PD." I showed her my ID.

She glanced quickly at it, nodded, then said, "You're looking for Nate, aren't you?"

I felt my heart rate multiply, almost like I was going into AFib, not that I'd ever had that experience, but you know what I mean, right?

"Why would you say that?" I asked. "Who are you?"

"My name is Bobbie Lynn Wilkesen," she said, extending her hand. I wasn't sure which reached me first, the alcohol on her breath, smoke from her cigarette, or her hand. It was a safe assumption that Bobbie Lynn Wilkesen had been drinking for a while.

I shook her hand politely. She didn't really grip my hand, just my fingers in a very feminine way. Her nails were acrylic and her hands were very soft, yet the signs of age were creeping into them. Her knuckles were deeply wrinkled and there were dark spots on the backs of her hands and wrists.

"I read in the papers about that man who died," she said quietly, taking a huge drag on the cigarette, then tapped it over the ashtray with her forefinger, sending a shower of sparks into the overflowing pile of butts. "He was in here you know. Tuesday afternoon. I saw him. He was talking with Nate. Nate isn't a nice person."

"Really?" I said. Then I showed Bobbie Lynn the two photos of both men and asked her to confirm that we were talking about the same people.

"Oh, yeah, that's him, and that's Nate. I know who he is, and I know who he will be, too." She stubbed out her cigarette and took a new one from a silver beaded cigarette case full of those long, thin cigarettes. They're usually packaged in pastel-colored boxes with the slogan, "You've come a long way, baby."

I frowned. "What can you tell me?"

"Nate has issues," Bobbie Lynn said as she lit the cigarette and took a long, deep drag. Then she turned her head and blew a stream of smoke away from me.

"Issues? What do you mean, issues? And how d'you know about them?" I asked.

"Let's just say I knew him before he changed. It was the Army that did it to him, the Marines," she said and gestured to Mickey.

He nodded, made her a drink of some dark liquor and a mixer, added a cherry, and brought it to her.

"Nate was in the Army?" I asked, as Mickey set the drink down on the table in front of her.

"No," Mickey said. "He's a Marine."

"This guy was in the Marines?" I held up the picture from the surveillance footage. "He's too small."

Every Marine I've ever known was huge and had an

even bigger ego. I'd heard recruitment was down but come on, really?

"He's five-eight and tough as shit," Mickey said. "Yeah. He was in the Marines. And then he was out of the Marines. Except, they're never out of the Marines, are they? Once a Marine, always a Marine." He rolled his eyes. "The guy is full of shit. He got kicked out when they found out what he was there for."

What the hell are they talking about?

I looked at Mickey and then to Bobbie Lynn.

"You have no compassion, Mickey," Bobbie Lynn said.

"Compassion isn't what Nate needs. He... What the hell am I saying... SHE! She needs a swift kick where the sun don't shine!" Mickey smirked down at me.

Me? I felt like an anvil had just fallen on my head.

"What?" was all I could utter.

"Yeah. That's right," Mickey said, so obviously enjoying himself. "He's a she, a woman, a girl, a female. And when she comes in here, most of my customers get antsy because she gives off a bad vibe. Not only that, but she doesn't have two nickels to rub together, and she's always on the hunt for new faces to buy her a round."

"This is a woman?" I held up the picture again. "You're sure?"

"He's going to be mad as hell when he hears you're still talking about him that way," Bobbie Lynn said to Mickey.

"Why do you keep saying he?" I asked, bewildered.

"What's he going to do about it? I'm not going to lie to the police. He's a she who wants to be a man... Look," Mickey said, looking down at me, "I don't care what people do, how they do it, or what frickin' gender they are or want to be. I'm just a bartender. But when someone starts hassling the customers or making people feel uneasy, then that interrupts business. And when that happens, I have to say something."

"You said Nate had issues," I said to Bobbie Lynn. "Is what Mickey said true? That at birth he was a... female?"

"I'm just saying he's got issues. He has a temper, and he has a chip on his shoulder," she replied, picking her teeth nervously with her manicured nails. "I think he wants so badly to be something he isn't that he overcompensates, and because of all that, he starts trouble with people."

"You didn't answer the question," Ann, who'd now joined me at the table, said. "Is he a woman?"

She looked away, obviously not wanting to answer.

"Yes he is, she is... Damn, you've got me going now," Mickey answered for her. "She's still a woman, yes!"

"When was the last time you saw him, her?" I looked at Mickey and then at Bobbie Lynn.

"The night that guy was killed," Mickey said.

Bobbie Lynn nodded.

"Did he... she say anything out of the ordinary?" I asked.

"Are you kidding?" Mickey said. "She says the same horseshit every time she comes in. She's making progress with her hormones. Her doctors have never seen anyone respond so well to treatment. Bullshit! She looks the same today as she did a year ago. Frankly, I don't think she's seeing any doctors. I think she's just playing dress-up."

I couldn't believe what I was hearing. I'd spent the last several days looking for a needle in a haystack, and the first solid identification I get comes from two people telling me I've been wrong all along? That my man is a woman? Hell, I needed a drink and I was about to ask Mickey for one when the door opened.

Mickey and Bobbie Lynn both looked around and then they froze.

"Son of a bitch," Mickey said. "Speak of the devil."

I turned, so did Ann. Nate had just waltzed in wearing the same camouflage jacket and baggy jeans he'd been wearing in my photo and was jauntily heading for the bar, his shoulders swaying from side to side.

"Shit!" Ann said. "That's him. That's Brown."

What happened next took no more than a couple of seconds.

I jumped to my feet, headed in the same direction, and said, "Excuse me. Can I talk to you for a minute?"

"Who, me?" Nate said, nervously, and began inching back and toward the door.

"Yes, just a quick word." I smiled... well, I thought I did, but I think it may have been more grimace than smile. I held up my ID and said, "I'm Detective Gazzara, Chattanooga Police."

"Oh, yeah. Cool. Uhm, yeah, okay. Just give me a sec while I go tell my ride that I'll be a few minutes," and she bolted toward the door. Yeah, it took less than ten seconds and he, she, whatever, was gone.

I ran after her, out through the front door. I stopped outside, listening. I heard the sound of feet running fast to my right. I ran after her, my weapon in hand, my heart pounding as the adrenaline surged through my body. She turned right into an alley. I was less than twenty yards behind her, the sweat already beading on my face.

And then I made a rookie mistake, and the next ten seconds almost cost me my life.

As I ran after her, I was trying to process what the hell and who the hell I was chasing. So instead of slowing down and taking precautions, I continued running headlong around the corner and into an empty alley, or so it seemed. And then it hit me, literally. Something slammed into the back of my head. I went down and my forehead hit the ground, hard.

I felt hands on me. I tried to roll over, my gun still in my hand. Something slammed into my ribs, and then a boot crashed down onto my wrist. The Glock flew out of my hand. The weight of the boot on my wrist increased. I tried to roll. I couldn't.

"Keep still, damn it," she snarled. "Don't frickin' move. I don't want to hurt you, but I will," she said.

Then the weight lifted off my wrist and she got in one last kick to my gut. It knocked the wind completely out of me. I lay there gasping for breath. Then I heard footsteps, running, and I was afraid she was coming back. With a supreme effort, a grunt, and a couple painful gasps, I reached out, grabbed the Glock, rolled up onto one knee, my weapon in one hand, the other cradling my ribs. I could still breathe. *Maybe I don't have any broken ribs,* I thought.

"Whoa, don't shoot. It's me!" Ann yelled as she ran toward me with Mickey close behind her.

Ann ran on past me, weapon in hand. Then, realizing Nate was gone, she stopped and bent, her hands on her knees, breathing hard. "Damn," I heard her say to herself, "I need some frickin' exercise. This is ridiculous." Then she turned and came back.

"You okay, Kate?" she asked, as Mickey took one of my arms and helped me up.

"No," I said. "I got stomped on and hit in the head. I hurt all over."

"You need to sit for a minute," Mickey said. "C'mon, I'll give you a hand." And he did, he took my arm and we returned to The Sovereign.

The place had emptied, all but for the crinkled old guy with the Dumbo ears. He was still working on his drink.

"Geez, where'd everybody go?" I asked, wincing.

"You sort of scared them off," Mickey said, grinning. "The people we get in here like to stay out of sight, if you get my meaning."

"That I do," I replied. "That I do."

"You look like you need a drink, Detective, both of you." He looked at Ann. She shook her head. "Detective?" he asked. "I won't tell if you don't, and I know old Ralph won't, right, Ralph?"

The crinkled old guy grinned hugely and shook his head.

"Thanks, but no thanks," I said. "But I will take a glass of water."

"Coming right up." Mickey turned away, grabbed a large tumbler, and went down the bar to fill it with ice.

"Her name is Nate Cassidy," the crinkled man called Ralph said.

"What's that?" I said softly.

"Nate Cassidy. Her real name is Natalie. I heard her talking once when she didn't think anyone was paying any attention," Ralph said, taking a sip of his drink. He winked at me and then went back to his brooding.

"Thanks, Ralph," I replied quietly.

Mickey returned and handed me my water. I drank about half of it down then asked for the lady's room.

"I'll be just a minute," I told Ann.

She nodded, then said, "Take it easy, okay? You want me to come with you?"

I shook my head and left her sitting at the bar. I could feel the goose egg already beginning to grow on my fore-head. *Shit!* I thought as I made my way to the restroom. *This is all I need.*

And the lady's room at The Sovereign did nothing to boost a girl's mood. The mirror over the sinks and the flores-cent light above the three stalls and the green paint on the walls made my skin look beyond sickly. *Geez, I look like a freaking zombie.*

The greenish tinge to my skin contrasted with the cut and trickle of blood at my hairline. My shirt, the thighs and backside of my pants, my palms, and my right cheek all had some kind of unnamable grime on them. God only knew how many patrons from The Sovereign had vomited in that alley or used it as a bathroom. My stomach flipped at the thought.

I brushed the crap off my clothes as best I could, washed my face, scrubbed my hands, dried off, and stared again into the mirror. My face, now devoid of makeup, looked back at me, and I shuddered. I sure as hell didn't want to be seen out in public looking like I did. I wanted to get out of there, in a hurry, go home, take a long hot shower, but I had little choice. I needed to find out who and what the hell this woman was.

19

I had Ann take me back to the PD, and I went to the locker room where I showered and cleaned myself up as best I could. There was little I could do about my clothes, but I always keep a couple of pairs of jeans and tops in my locker so I changed, threw the dirties on the locker floor and slammed the door shut on them. Some lipstick, a little foundation, and a touch of blush worked wonders on my face, or so I thought.

By the time I was done prissing and primping, it was after five. I wanted to go home, but I didn't. I needed to talk to Janet. One, I wanted to make sure she was okay. Two, I wanted to compare notes. Following the dynamic shift in the focus of the case, I wanted to see if I could jog her memory, so I again headed to the hospital.

I didn't go through the emergency room entrance. Instead I parked in the multi-story lot and went straight to her room on the second floor.

"Knock-knock," I said as I entered.

"Oh wow, Kate," she said. "What happened to you?" *So much for the makeup!*

"Not much. How're you feeling?"

"Better. I can't wait to get out of here... You look like you were hit by a truck. So what happened?"

"Geez, Janet. Thank you for the kind words."

"Oh, oh no. I didn't mean... I'm sorry, I just—"

"I know," I said. "I was kidding, okay? You're right about the truck, though, well, sort of. It's been quite a day. Where's Adam, by the way?"

"Doctor Joon sent him home. So tell me. What happened?"

"We found the guy who did this to you, is what happened. Well, we think it was him, but as yet there's no proof of anything. I'm hoping you can help."

"Oh, Lord. You arrested him, right? He's in custody?"

"No! He got away. I was chasing him down... Hey, it's good to see that you're feeling better."

"I am. In fact I'd like to get out of here, but they want to keep me for at least another day... Kate, did you really think it was necessary to put a uniform outside my door?"

"That was the Chief's idea," I said as I made myself comfortable on the edge of her bed and took out my mini recorder. "So, Sergeant Toliver," I said, smiling at her, "you know the routine. Start at the beginning. Tell me what happened."

"I've already told you most of it," she said. "Adam and I were supposed to meet at that bar, Second Base, where Logan had been spotted. I hadn't planned anything. We were just going to have a beer and get the lay of the land, maybe ask a question or two, show Logan's photo around. I knew Ann and Miller had already covered the place, but it was a date and something to do. I'd just gotten out of the car when bam, and that's about all I know."

"Did you get a look at him? Did you see anything at all?"

"Aha! Yeah, it came to me earlier today. I was trying to remember what happened and I... well, you remember I told you his partner had a tattoo on the back of her hand? It was one of those blue things, a jailhouse tat. It was a Marine badge. You know, the anchor and globe thing... Look, the guy who jumped me only got the upper hand because I didn't see him coming. If I had, things would have been different. He'd be in my place right now, and a lot worse off than me, I can tell you that." Janet shook her head.

"You didn't get a look at his face?"

"No."

"How big was he?"

"Hm, not hugely big, in good shape... I guess."

"What about his hair?"

She shook her head. "No. I didn't see it... Kate, what is it? You look like you know more than you're saying."

Before I could answer and tell Janet the full story, Doctor Napai entered the room.

"Visitors at this hour?" she said and clicked her tongue disapprovingly. "She needs to rest... What happened to you?"

She took a penlight from her coat breast pocket, put her hand on my head, and pulled it toward her.

"I'm okay, Doctor," I said. "It's just part of the job."

"No," she said, sternly. "It's not okay. This is a nasty

bump. And..." She rubbed the back of my head, making me pull back and wince. "You also have another bump here."

She let go of my head, took a step back, folded her arms, and glared up at me. If I hadn't been in the state I was, I would have found it funny. She was about the size of a thirteen-year-old girl—I towered over her. But there I was, standing in front of her, feeling like an idiot.

"Captain," she said, "you need to have your head properly examined."

"I've been told that on more than one occasion," I joked nervously. "I'm okay, doc, really I am. I promise. How about I come back when I get done... with my work. I mean, I have to go back to the police department, and well, there's paperwork I have to finish, so it might take me a while, I mean..." I could see she wasn't buying it. "I will. I'll come and let you take a look, doctor. I promise."

She snorted, fussed around Janet for a minute, checked her chart, gifted me with a look that would have frozen a waterfall, then left, shaking her finger at me.

"Wow! She scares the hell out of me," I said when she'd gone.

"That's only because you know she's right," Janet replied.

I rubbed the back of my head as if to say *See, no big deal,* but I wasn't fooling anyone; it hurt like hell, but I ignored Janet's look of concern and continued.

"So, back to our perp," I said, and then I relayed to her all that had happened over the past few hours, the short version, of course, and then I dropped the bomb. "Brown is not Brown. She's Natalie Cassidy."

Janet looked stunned. "What? Are you telling me it was a woman who did this to me?"

"I can't say for sure, but it sure looks like it," I said.

"Are you... You're not sure? Wow!" she stuttered.

"Not yet," I said, "but we're working on it. As far as we can tell, she's the last person to see Jack Logan alive. She was seen talking to him, and we have it on video, not more than thirty minutes before he died. According to the bartender and the Wilkesen woman, this Cassidy person is taking some kind of hormones and seeing a doctor for a gender swap."

"I want to help," she said, obviously excited. "I need to get out of here."

"No you don't," I said. "You need to take it easy and get well. We have her name. Miller will track her down, get her background and an address, and we need to find that doctor. Sheesh, how many shrinks can there be who handle this gender transformation thing?"

By the time I got out of the hospital, the pain at the back of my eyes was killing me. I blamed it on the bright lights, but I knew what was really happening: a migraine. Every once in a while, usually in stressful situations, I'd get a real humdinger and they all started the same way, at the back of my eyes.

The idea of quitting for the day was sounding better and better; it was, after all, almost six-thirty. But I had to stop off at the PD and talk to my people. What I didn't know at the time was that Doctor Joon was right, and I was in trouble. As I was driving back to Amnicola, I missed several turns and had to back-track. I'd driven that route, back and forth, a thousand times, but now... Well, I just couldn't stay focused. Finally, though, I pulled into the parking lot at the front of the PD, shut off the engine, let out a deep breath, and laid my head back against the headrest: not a good idea. Pain speared through my head like a red-hot knife.

I sat for a minute, my eyes closed, waiting for the pain to subside. Then I stepped out of the car, made it into the building, took the elevator to the second floor, and from there to the incident room where I found Miller still at his desk. I'd forgotten what my face looked like until I saw the expression on his face.

"Hey Cap," he said. "Ann said you'd gotten into a kafuffle, but she wouldn't elaborate. What the hell happened to you?"

"That's what she told you, huh?" I said, unaware I was rubbing the back of my head. "You should see the other guy."

"Did you make a bust?" Miller asked, not catching my joke.

"No. I'm the one who got busted... upside the back of my head." Involuntarily, I rubbed it and winced.

"Your eyes are all... You're not well, Cap. I'll call the Chief," he said and turned and reached for his desk phone.

"Whoa! Stop! Do *not* call the Chief. That's an order. If he finds out he'll take me off the case, and I can't have that, not when we're about to crack it wide open." I closed my eyes, breathed deeply, pinching the bridge of my nose.

"Well, okay, but—"

"No buts," I said. "We keep it to ourselves, okay?"

"Okay, but you went to see Janet at the hospital. Did they check you out while you were there?"

"Oh come on, Miller, you're not my moth-er. Oh shit. I'm sorry. Yeah, Janet's doctor checked me out." It wasn't a total lie, but a little voice at the back of my head was telling me that I was doing the wrong thing. As usual, I ignored it.

"Look," I said, "I just wanted to bring you and Hawk up to speed, let you know what Ann and I found out. Specifically, that the guy we're looking for is a woman."

"No way! I think you must have hit your head harder than you think."

"Nope," I said. "I'm serious. Look, I need everything you can find on a Natalie Cassidy. She's ex-military, so there should be a record. She certainly has a history of psychological problems. I also want to know who she works for, where she lives, and who she lives with. Your priority, though, is to find me the address. I have to take this monster off the streets."

"You got it. But first, I'm going to take you home. It's past quitting time, and you need to rest up." And before I could refuse, he was on his feet, keys in hand.

Any other day, I would have made a fuss and told him to get off my back, but I didn't. I knew he was right. I let him drive me home. He got me there in no time and parked his car at the door.

"I'll walk you to the door," he said.

"We're not on a date, Miller. I can get into my apartment," I grumbled.

"Okay, but I'll wait here until you get inside."

"Fine. Thanks," I muttered ungratefully as I opened the car door and stepped out into the darkness and the rain.

I pulled my collar up around my neck and hurried up

the steps and heard him say through his open window, "You're welcome, Cap."

I waved my hand dismissively, unlocked my front door, stepped inside, and closed the door.

Later, I'd be sorry that I'd been such an ass.

20

I was never so happy to get behind closed doors in my life. I didn't even turn on the lights in my apartment. I stood for a minute, leaning back against the front door, and allowed my eyes to adjust to the darkness. Then I turned and slipped the deadbolt into place. The green numbers of my iWatch read seven-oh-two.

I went to my bedroom, peeled off my clothes, slipped into bed and within minutes was sound asleep, but it wasn't even twenty minutes later when my phone rang. I thought my world had exploded, and even though the room was totally dark, I had to squint my eyes as I picked up the phone.

"Gazzara," I muttered.

"What the hell, Catherine? I just heard that you have a head injury and that you haven't seen a doctor," the male voice shouted, making my head ring.

"Mom, is that you?" I said, knowing it was Chief Johnston, but I just couldn't help myself.

"Don't be smart with me, Gazzara!"

"All right, Chief," I said, now fully awake. "I'm sorry. Look, I did see a doctor. I just didn't... I promised I'd see her again later. I'm fine. I just got a little banged up, is all. I'm okay, really I am." I pushed myself up onto one elbow.

"Bull. Miller will pick you up. He said you'd be pissed at him for letting me know you got jumped," the Chief barked at me. "I told him not as pissed as I am that you didn't get yourself checked out!"

"Chief, I've got some news you need to hear about the Logan case—"

"I don't want to hear a damn thing about it until you've been cleared by a doctor," he growled, interrupting me.

"Ok. I'll go with Miller and get myself checked out." I sighed.

"And don't even think of setting foot in this department without a doctor's note. I mean it, Kate. Don't screw with me." I could see in my mind the Chief's teeth clenched and his left eye twitching.

"Yes, sir." But there was a click as he hung up. He didn't say good-bye. *Damn! I should have seen this coming. What was I thinking?*

I took a deep breath and carefully crawled out of bed, trying not to move my head too much. My headache was almost gone, but I figured there was no point in pushing my luck: I still had a tiny spear sticking into the back of my right eyeball.

I took a quick shower, dressed in my sweats, grabbed my purse, badge and Glock, and headed to the front door. I figured that Miller should already be pulling up outside. I couldn't wait to hear his excuse, and apology, for ratting on me and then insisting he did it for my own good. I knew it was, and that his intentions were good, but I still felt like I didn't need a damn babysitter. And then I began to wonder if maybe I'd forgotten what it felt like to have someone who actually gave a shit about me.

I grimaced, knowing that if it was true, it was because I chose it that way. The life I lived wasn't conducive to close friendships, close relationships. Let's face it; there's nothing more dangerous than a policewoman with a weapon on her hip and a broken heart beneath her badge.

I knew Miller was just looking out for me. Janet would have done the same.

I opened the front door. *Where the hell is he?*

It was raining outside and bone-chilling cold. I closed the door and waited, watching the parking lot through the window at the top of the door, and I waited.

Ten minutes later Miller still hadn't arrived, and I was getting seriously pissed. I took out my phone and called him. His phone rang four times then went to voicemail.

"What are you thinking, Kate?" I muttered to myself. *It's a horrible night, and he's driving, so he's not going to pick up the phone and risk an accident. Not Lennie Miller.*

So I hung around the front door, checking the parking lot every couple of seconds through the window, but time continued to tick by and there was still no Miller. I was beginning to panic, thinking he must have had an accident or something. I called him again; still no answer, so I called the Chief.

"What now, Catherine?"

"He hasn't shown up," I said. "You did tell him to come here, right? Could he have misunderstood and gone... Hell, I don't know; he's not answering his phone, Chief."

"No. He offered to pick you up at your place," Johnston said in a low voice.

"Maybe he's had an accident," I said.

"I doubt it. It's been almost an hour. We would have heard something from the emergency services."

"Right... that's right," I said, thinking. "Okay, I guess I'll drive myself to the hospital. It's not a big deal—"

"You'll stay right where you are. I'll send a unit. In the meantime, keep trying to raise Miller on his phone. I'll try his apartment." The line went dead.

I called Miller again, still no answer. I was beginning to have a really bad feeling that something had happened to him.

Finally, I saw a blue and white cruiser turning in through the gates and I stepped outside. It had stopped raining, so I paused on the top step and hit redial. I put the phone to my ear and heard his phone begin to ring... and then I heard his ring tone. *What the hell?*

I hit the red stop button and then the redial again. Sure enough, somewhere close by I could hear Miller's phone ringing; it was faint, but that's what it was, I was sure of it, the theme from Star Wars, what else?

"What the hell?" I muttered out loud as the uniformed officer got out of the car.

"Good evening, Detective. Chief sent me to—"

"Yeah, I know, to take me to the hospital. Stand still for just a second and listen." I hit the redial again. "Do you hear a cell phone ringing?"

"Yes, ma'am." He looked to the left of the lot, then pointed and said, "That way."

My apartment is an end unit. The parking lot circles the

block. My front door faces north, my living room window faces east. Miller's car was parked under my window on the east side of the building. Its driver's side window open and I could see he was asleep at the wheel.

"Miller!" I shouted. "What the hell? The Chief is going to skin us both alive! How could you fall—"

"Oh shit," the officer said from the driver's side of Miller's car. And he grabbed his radio. "Officer down, officer down!"

I ran around the car, stopped, both hands to my mouth, staring in through the open window, the bile boiling up into my mouth. I was sure I was about to throw up.

Miller had been shot in the left temple, through the open driver's side window. His jacket was open and his wallet was on the ground beside the car. My mind went blank. I could see nothing but the wound at the side of his head. It seemed to grow bigger and bigger as I stared at it. I tried to go to him, but the officer grabbed me and held me back.

"Hold on, Detective," he said as I struggled to break loose. "There's nothing you can do for him."

"*I need to help him,*" I screamed. "*Where the hell are the paramedics?*"

They arrived a few minutes later, lights flashing, siren blaring, along with several police cruisers.

I watched as an ambulance careened into the complex, screeched to a stop, and three paramedics jumped out and ran to the car.

With deadpan expressions on their faces, they went quickly to work only to stop again almost immediately and turn away; there was nothing they could do for him. And I knew then that there was no hope of resuscitating Miller. And then the tears came. I tried to hold them back, but I couldn't. It's not good for a woman police officer to be seen crying in public. It looks weak, especially when there are male officers around, but I couldn't help it. I just stood there, my right elbow supported by my left hand, my right fist in my mouth, the tears rolling down my cheeks.

Miller was dead, no doubt about it, and I knew it was my fault. If I had done the right thing and had myself properly checked out, he would have been back at the office doing his thing on his computer instead of sitting in his car outside my apartment with his brains blown out.

What the hell was wrong with me? When was I ever going to learn? My eyes stung and my headache was back.

I stood there, watching as more and more officers arrived, everyone around me moving, at least to me, as if in slow motion. None of it was registering. How could a member of my team be dead? *My* team.

"Kate?" I heard a quiet voice behind me say.

I turned. It was Doc Sheddon.

"It's my fault, Doc."

"No. It isn't. It's the fault of the person who pulled the trigger," Doc said, but I was having none of it.

"How am I going to tell his mom?" I asked, more for something to say than for an answer. "He was everything to her. How am I going to face her and tell her it was my fault? I don't think I can do it."

"Yes, you can," he replied. "You'll do it the way you do everything else, Kate. Now, I suggest you get out of here and let us do our jobs."

That's what I should have done, but I didn't.

Out of the corner of my eye, I saw a red Monte Carlo drive through the gate. It parked beyond the tapes and Ann jumped out and ran to us, ducking under the tapes. I quickly turned away so she couldn't see my tears. I wiped my eyes; not that it could have done much good, they must have been as red as... Well, you get the idea.

"Cap? Is it true?" she shouted, as she stopped short, a good two car lengths away from where we were standing. It was like she didn't want to get any nearer to the crime scene for fear that might make it all the more real. That maybe, if she stood far enough away, Miller would somehow be all right. I knew exactly how she felt, but all I could do was nod my head.

"I heard it over the radio," she said. "I can't believe it." She began to pace back and forth, constantly wiping her eyes as she watched the paramedics slowly packing up their gear.

Doc squeezed my shoulder as he left me and went to Miller. I followed him, wanting to get another look at the friend who'd driven me home just a short while ago, this time as a professional. It wasn't easy. I had to block out the personal stuff and see it for what it was, a crime scene and a victim. It wasn't quite the same as Logan or any of the three other cases. Lennie had been shot only once, but in the left temple. It looked similar to me.

I stood back, away from the car, looked around at my apartment building. It was like I was seeing it for the first time. Lennie's car was right under my window. Why hadn't I heard the shot? Why had no one heard the shot? There were people gathering now beyond the tapes, staring... at me. Most of them were my neighbors and knew what I did for a living. I hated to think what might have been going through their heads that night. Nothing good, of that I was certain.

I turned and looked at the building opposite mine. It was just across the street, maybe thirty yards away. All of the widows had drapes; all the drapes were closed. Nobody could have seen anything unless they were peeping, and why would they be? All I needed was one person, just one person... and then I spotted it: a blue light next to the front door of a ground floor apartment, not quite opposite mine, but two doors up on the other side of the street, about forty yards away.

That's a frickin' doorbell camera. Nah, I couldn't get that lucky, could I?

"Ann, I think that's a doorbell camera over there," I said, pointing. "I know the owner."

"Let's go," she said without looking at Miller's car.

Together, we hurried across the street and... it was, it was a doorbell cam. *Yes!*

I rang the bell and we waited.

21

It took Mr. Himel, my neighbor across the road, about ten minutes to contact his security company and download the footage to his laptop.

"Detective, I am so sorry for your loss," he said as we waited for the huge file to download, more than three hours of it, all the way back to ten minutes before Miller dropped me off at just before seven o'clock that evening. Finally, it was done. With a couple taps on the keyboard and a few clicks of his mouse, he cued up the small window of time when I knew for a fact that Miller was still alive.

I had to choke down my feelings as I watched the video. Ann, I think, was also having trouble, but I didn't look at her to find out.

The quality of the image wasn't bad, but it wasn't great either, and we were dealing with a distance of more than forty yards, but it was enough, just.

We watched as I got out of Miller's car and went to my front door. Sure enough, like a good Boy Scout, he waited until I was in the building before pulling away... except that he didn't pull away. Instead, he backed out of the parking space and pulled around to the east side of the building, then stopped in a parking spot under my window.

"That must have been when he called the Chief," I muttered.

"Can I ask what you guys were doing?" Ann asked.

As we watched, I gave her the short version of what had happened when I arrived back at the PD. How Miller had insisted on taking me home. Again feelings of guilt almost overwhelmed me.

"Wait until I get my hands on the freakin' bitch," Ann whispered as the footage continued to roll.

As I watched, I continually checked the time stamp at the bottom of the screen. At seven-oh-eight, I leaned closer to the computer screen and squinted. A minute later, at seven-oh-nine a shadow, someone running, slipped around the back of the car to the driver's side door. For a moment we saw nothing. It was her, though; there was just enough light from the window next to mine for me to tell. She was leaning forward, bent low. I figured she must have been talking to him. And then there was a tiny flash of bright light.

Shit! That's a muzzle flash, but she's using a suppressor. No wonder no one heard the shot.

And then nothing, at least for a moment, and then the shadow was off and running, fast. It hopped over the fence and ran across the empty scrub between the complex and the mini-mall on Brainerd Road.

"Freakin' hell." Ann slapped the table. "Are you freakin' serious?"

"It was her, Ann," I said quietly. "Nate, Natalie Cassidy

didn't figure on us catching her on a doorbell cam." I felt the bile rise again in the back of my throat; this time I was in trouble.

As calmly as possible, I asked Himel if I could use his bathroom. As soon as I closed and locked the door, I turned on the faucet, lifted the toilet lid, dropped to my knees and heaved. There was nothing much in my stomach but my body still insisted on trying to expel my guts. After what seemed like an hour, but was probably less than a couple of minutes, and with my stomach in a knot, I was finally able to stand upright again.

I washed my hands and face and tried to pull myself together, but the problem was that no matter how hard I tried, I couldn't get past the idea that what had happened to Miller was my fault. If only... yeah, well, you know what they say about if only, right?

There was a knock on the door.

"Hey, Cap? You all right in there?" Ann asked.

"Yeah," I lied. "I'll be right out."

22

It was midnight before Ann left on that terrible evening of Friday the 13th. Doc was long gone and he'd taken poor Lennie with him—that was one autopsy I would not be attending. The crime scene unit was still there when I went to bed after Ann left, and they were still there the following morning.

I didn't get much sleep that night, what was left of it. I tossed and turned, watched the clock, then sometime around two o'clock I fell into a sort of half-life: half asleep and half awake. And I dreamed, oh how I dreamed. I must have watched, close-up, a dozen times as the woman shot Lennie in the head.

I woke early the next morning just before six-thirty... Hah, I never was really asleep. I called and scheduled an Uber for seven forty-five. Then I showered, dressed, drank four cups of coffee in the space of less than an hour, and then, trying to push aside the headache that lay waiting in the dark backroads of my brain, I gathered up my gear and went outside to wait for the Uber. I arrived at the police department a few minutes before eight o'clock.

The mood in the situation room was somber... No, it was downright dismal. The place was packed with uniforms and detectives. Word had spread throughout the department about the demise of Detective Lennie Miller. Conversations were being conducted in hushed voices. Heads were held a little lower over the desks. Phone calls were being answered a little slower. And I was conscious of the sidelong glances I was getting from just about every officer present. It was a nightmarish situation, and I'd never experienced anything like it before. Sure, officers had died in the line of duty before, but somehow this one was different; Lennie had a lot of friends.

The only people who didn't feel the melancholy were the criminals who were being brought in. They got yelled at just a little louder than usual, treated a little rougher by officers who already had short tempers, and there wasn't a damn thing that anyone could do about it. It was a bad day; one of the worst I'd ever experienced, and it wasn't about to improve.

So, when I walked into the situation room that morning, all eyes were upon me; not a good feeling, and I wondered what everyone was thinking. Was I being blamed for Lennie's death? It wouldn't have surprised me. But then came the outpouring of sympathy and good wishes, for which I was grateful, but didn't make me feel any better.

Lennie's desk had already been cleaned off. His laptop was gone, his chair was pushed tidily under his desk, and I... felt like shit. Hawk and Ann had not yet arrived, and Janet was still in the hospital. For several moments I stood there alone, then I pulled Lennie's chair out from under his desk and sat down on it, stretched out my legs, laid a hand on the desktop, closed my eyes, and drummed slowly on it with the tips of my fingers. I remember nothing of the next ten minutes or so.

And it must have been at least ten minutes later when I felt a presence behind me. I turned my head and looked up. I didn't need to. I knew who it was, and I also knew I wasn't even supposed to be there. I should have been either in bed or at the hospital getting my head examined. Doctor Joon had never uttered truer words.

"My office, now," Chief Johnston said.

I rose to my feet. Ann, who had just arrived, grabbed me and hugged me, and then whispered in my ear that it would be okay and gently patted me on the back, and walked on over to her desk.

I heard Hawk speaking to someone too. Who it was or what they were talking about, I don't remember, but I do remember that I didn't care.

"Chief," I said as I followed him into his office. "I know I'm not supposed to be here, but I—"

"Shut up and sit down, Kate," he said and walked slowly around behind his desk and sat down.

I did as I was told. I said not a word—nor did he—as I watched him open the bottom desk drawer, reach inside, and take out a bottle of Jack Daniels and two double shot glasses. He unscrewed the cap, poured one and placed it at the edge of his desk in front of me, then poured the other and set the bottle down.

"To Lennie," he said and raised his shot glass.

"To Lenn..." My voice trailed off. I grabbed the glass and tossed the double measure back in one hit. I almost choked as the fiery liquid burned its way down the back of my throat. I closed my eyes and waited, and slowly my head began to clear.

"Kate," Johnston said, replacing the bottle in the drawer, "this is the kind of situation where nothing I can say, or anyone else can say, will bring you any comfort. But the one thing you have to know and understand is—and I'll never stop telling each and every one of you—this is not your fault."

I felt the tears begin to well up, and I bit the inside of my mouth, trying to fight them off. Somehow I managed it, but I knew that he knew.

"It's the bad guy's fault," he continued. "This sack of excrement is who's to blame for what he did to Lennie. And we'll find him, Kate," he hissed. "You'll find him."

"Her," I said quietly.

"What?"

"It's not a male. It's a woman. We have her on surveillance footage from a doorbell camera. It's not really clear enough to recognize her, but I know it's her. It was the same woman who put me down yesterday, too. And she's our serial killer. She's transgender. Goes by the name Nate Cassidy. Her real name's Natalie. That's what I wanted to tell you last night before you sent me home."

"You're sure about all this?" the Chief asked.

"Yea," I said, staring down into the now empty glass. "I'm sure. I talked to some of her... acquaintances; I don't think she has any friends. None that I know of, anyway." I was waffling, trying to put my thoughts in order, but I couldn't. I figured it must have been the Jack Daniels.

"Anyway," I continued, "that's what came up. I don't have all the details yet, but I'll get it done. You can count on that. Her friends claimed that she was seeing a doctor for her *reassignment* procedure." I spat the word out like I'd spat out the bile at the Himel residence the previous night. *Freakin' bitch. I'll reassign you, to the freakin' grave.*

"Kate," Johnston said. "I know this is not going to go down well, but I need you to take a step back."

"What? Why? Oh no. Not now. Not after Lennie... You can't do this to me."

"I can, and I must, and especially now after what happened to Detective Miller. You can either do as I ask, or I'll suspend you. Either way, you'll leave your badge and gun here with me."

"Oh come on, Chief. Please don't do this... You can't do this to me. Every one of my team is suffering. We have to catch this monster. We have to find her, and fast. She's dangerous. If she was at my apartment building, she must have been looking for... me."

I knew I'd been babbling, but that thought struck me dumb. I stared at the Chief then grabbed my glass and said, "I need another."

He obliged. I tossed it back like it was nothing and yes, I know, it wasn't even nine o'clock yet.

"That's it, isn't it?" I asked. "She was waiting for me. She didn't expect Miller to give me a ride home and wait while I went inside. And she killed him, Chief. She knew I was onto her, and she decided to stop me." I wasn't sure if it was the Jack Daniels or the weight of the situation, but I was suddenly overwhelmed by a serious case of the jitters.

"All of that makes sense," he said. "But how? How did she know you were all working the Logan case? It can't be just dumb luck."

"From the incident at The Sovereign, probably. I questioned several people there. She's a regular, right? Other than that... I don't know, Chief. I can't think of anything else."

"Kate, you're babbling; you're not thinking clearly, and that's because of the crack on the head." He paused, stared at me.

I knew what was coming and shook my head so violently it hurt.

"I'm sending you to the doctor," he said, "and then you're going home to rest. That's it. No arguments."

"Chief, please."

"I said no arguments, and I'm sending the rest of your team home as well. Working in the state you all are in now is... well, it isn't going to change a thing. But a good night's rest and some food in your stomach will help. We now know who she is, so don't worry. There's nothing more you or your team can do. I'll have them put out an APB on this Nate... Natalie Cassidy person. We'll get him... her."

He leaned forward, folded his hands in front of him, and said, "You need help, and your team needs rest."

He picked up his desk phone, punched a button, and said, "Cathy, come in here please, and bring your notebook."

She came in almost immediately, notebook in hand.

Johnston looked at me and said, "I want the name of that neurosurgeon you talked to yesterday."

I sighed and told him.

"Cathy. Call the doctor. Use my name. I want her to see Captain Gazzara this morning, as soon as possible. Let me know."

Cathy nodded and left.

He punched in another number. "Charles, have a car brought round to the front, and then come and get Gazzara and take her to the hospital, and stay with her until she's seen the doctor. Don't let her out of your sight until the doctor's finished her examination, and then take her home. Make sure she gets safely inside, okay?"

He listened to whatever Charles replied, nodded, and hung up.

"Okay," I said, resigned to my fate. "You win."

He pointed to his desktop, and said, "Gun, badge."

Reluctantly, I handed them over.

"Now, get the hell out of here and don't come back without a release from the doctor."

I shook my head at him, rose to my feet, staggered a little, then turned and left his office, and boy was I ever pissed.

I did manage to pull myself together for my interview with Dr. Napai. I insisted I was fine, lied through my teeth in answer to her questions, complained that the Chief was just being an ass, and tried to get her to declare me fit for work. It was one of the best acts I'd ever put on, and she fell for it, sort of. She didn't do as I asked, though. Instead, she went along with the Chief's request and told me to go home and rest and made an appointment to see me again the following Friday. But said nothing about me going back to work.

In hindsight, it was in fact one of my worst acts of rebellion. Had I done as I was told; had I let her examine me properly, the course of events over the next several days might well have taken a different direction.

23

The next time we were gathered together in my office, two days later, after two days rest I neither wanted or needed, or so I thought, the whiteboard was no longer white. We had the photos of the other three suspected victims up there along with their autopsy photos, and those of Jack Logan. Unfortunately, they also included Miller's photos, and those of his killer. And she, Cassidy, was still at large. The Chief's APB hadn't produced a single sighting.

Me? I was relatively clear-headed and headache free, though I still wasn't over Miller's death, nor would I ever be. I just had to make sure I stayed out of the Chief's way. I didn't dare go ask for the return of my gun and badge for fear he'd send me home again.

It was Ann who had taken over from Miller, and she collated and printed out the information on our subject and then handed it out.

"Natalie Cassidy, or Nate Cassidy, as he likes to be

called, is who we are looking for," Ann said. "She's twenty-nine years old, brunette turned blond, five-seven, size nine shoes, or boots. She has no criminal record, but she was briefly in the Marine Corps, one of the few women fit and strong enough to make it through the selection process. She served about fourteen weeks before she received an ELS—Entry Level Separation."

"So, she's a Marine," I said. "Was a Marine, though I'm told there's no such thing. Ooh frickin' rah."

"ELS?" Hawk asked. "Do we know what happened?"

"If you can read through all the military jargon," Ann replied, "Natalie Cassidy, as she was when she enlisted, intended to use the military to get her... gender reassignment surgery, and it probably would have worked for her had she played by the rules. The problem was, it was all she was focused on. She couldn't, or wouldn't, keep up with the Marine Corps basic training. Oh she had what it takes physically, but not mentally. She didn't have the fortitude to carry it through. Her Sergeant's report indicates that they tried to help her, but her attitude made it impossible for her to continue. Let's face it, for a woman, joining the military is hard enough; joining the Corps is—"

"Ooh-rah," Hawk muttered, interrupting her.

"Even harder," Ann continued, glaring at him. "So, since she didn't get into any real trouble, and was just more of a thorn in their side, they gave her an out."

"Does she have any family?" I asked, thinking there might be somewhere she would run to if she found herself backed into a corner.

"She does, though her mother died when she was a

teenager back in oh-four. Her father is still alive and living in Norton, Texas, and has been for the past four years. According to military records and a psych evaluation, they didn't get along. But no report of abuse of any kind."

"Has anybody talked to him?" I asked.

"Yes, I did," Hawk said. "He claims he hasn't spoken to his daughter in more than two years." He shrugged. "But who knows? He sounded like a dumbass. We should probably follow up."

I nodded. It was something to think about.

"Anything else?" I asked.

"Oh, I haven't even gotten started," Ann said. "Janet's been making calls from home."

Geez, why am I not surprised?

"She called me. Apparently, Natalie's been seeing a specialist and a shrink. She's still trying to make the transition from female to male. Janet talked to her shrink, a Dr. Reginald Morgan—apparently, he's British—but he wouldn't discuss Cassidy; claimed doctor-patient confidentiality. The specialist, though, a Dr. Audrey Harmon, admitted that she'd met with Cassidy on three occasions and agreed to be interviewed. I made an appointment to see her at two this afternoon. You want to come with me?"

"Excellent, but d'you think you can handle it by yourself? Janet won't be back for at least a couple more days and—"

"You think?" Janet said as she barged into the office. "Count me in."

"Wow. Doctor Joon released you early?" I said.

"Yeah," she said, avoiding my eyes. "I told her what had

happened and that I needed to get back to work. She wasn't happy about it, but she released me... Okay, she did release me, really, but for light duties only. That's not going to cut it, Cap. I need to be in on this. I need to..." She paused, her lower lip trembled, than she sat down, opened her iPad and mumbled, "I need to work. Don't try to stop me."

"Welcome back, Janet," Hawk said. "Robar is just getting started."

"Ann has an appointment with Doctor Harmon this afternoon," I said to Janet. "You can go with her."

Ann folded her arms across her chest and rocked back and forth on her heels. "We also have a place of employment and an apartment," she continued. "I had officers check out both places, but she hasn't been seen at either one in more than a week."

"Why am I not surprised?" I said. "Where does she live and where does she work? Who's her boss?"

"She lives in an apartment off 23rd. She works at Happy Henry's Family Fun Center," Ann said, shaking her head. "Her boss is Happy Henry Pierce."

"Now why didn't we think to look there first?" Hawk said and slapped his thigh.

"Hawk, you can go interview Pierce, now," I said. "We can't go slow on this. We have to find her—before she kills again."

Hawk nodded, stood up, and adjusted his badge and gun.

"Any news on the DNA found in the car?" I asked.

"No. They're still working on it," he said, shaking his head.

"Okay," I said to him, "call me when you're done with Happy Henry. We'll need a warrant to search the apartment... Oh shit. That means I have to talk to the Chief. Never mind, I'll just have to bluff my way through it. I need to get my weapon and badge from him anyway." I took a deep breath, then continued, "Remember, emotions are high, and so they should be, but we can't afford to screw up. We have to do it by the book."

I paused, looked at Hawk, then at Janet, then at Ann, and continued, "I don't care what kind of issues this person has, she has to go down. We need a solid case so we can lock her up for good. But here's the thing..." I hesitated for a moment, because I knew what I was about to say, if it was leaked to the press, could cause problems; Internal Affairs would be all over it.

"This is a high-profile case. We have a serial killer, a woman with this special 'condition,'" I said, making air quotes with my fingers. "You can assume that she will land herself a lawyer who's looking to make a reputation. There will be no hole too tight, black, or dirty that he won't crawl through to say that we violated her rights. So we do it right, by the book, okay? Let's deliver Christmas to the Chief early this year."

They all nodded, collected their things and went to work. Cathy wasn't in her office, so I knocked on Chief Johnston's door and waited.

"Come in."

"Hey, Chief," I said. "It's me."

"Yes," he replied without looking up from the paperwork he was reading. "I heard you were back. I've been expecting you. How are you feeling?"

"I'm good." I swallowed noisily and continued, "I need a search warrant, Chief. Robar found a residence for Natalie Cassidy." I put the paperwork on his desk and stood back.

He looked up at me and said, "Kate, did you see the doctor as I asked?"

"I did. She checked me out and I went home and went to bed, just as you ordered. Now I'm fine, well-rested and back at it. Now—"

"The doctor's release please, Catherine," he said, holding out his hand.

"I... don't have it with me."

"Go get it."

"Chief, I need that warrant."

"I'll get you your warrant when you get me your doctor's release. Either that or I'll take you off this case until you do. Take your pick."

There were a million things I wanted to say. This was practically blackmail. I was being strong-armed by my own chief to do something that I didn't think needed to be done. I was furious, but I had to choke it down.

All I could say was, "Yes, sir." And I stood and walked out of the room. I was tempted to slam the door, but I didn't.

My car had been left at the station when the uniformed officer drove me home. So when I climbed in, windows rolled up, I screamed. I banged the steering wheel. I swore like only a trucker knows how. And then I called Dr. Joon.

Of course, I didn't get her. I got her nurse practitioner.

"I need to see her, now," I said belligerently: big mistake. "I'm a police officer. I need a release to go back to work."

"Your follow-up appointment's not until Friday," she said, even more belligerently than me.

"I know that," I snarled, "but I'm conducting a murder investigation. I need to go back to work, now!"

"I'm sorry, Captain. Doctor Napai has a full schedule. You'll have to wait for your appointment."

"Oh, come on... special circumstances, please... Can't you give me a release?"

"I'm sorry. I can't. And, as I said, the doctor has a full schedule. You'll have to wait until she sees you on Friday."

And she hung up, and I lost it. I banged my hands on the steering wheel and I screamed, and I screamed, and then I gave up and leaned back against the headrest and closed my eyes. I thought about what the hell I could possibly do to get myself out of the mess I'd gotten myself into. And then I did what anyone in my position would do. I called the one person who I knew could help.

"Doc, I need a favor."

Doc Sheddon and I have always had a special relationship—no, nothing like that. We were just... He was more than just the medical examiner who I worked with regularly; he was my friend. And at times like this... Well, I hate to say it, but he was also my accomplice.

"A doctor's note? Are you kidding? I can't do that. And, you are missing the crucial element that would allow me to see you professionally. You're still alive. Come on, Kate, you know I can't give you one. Johnston would take one look at it and toss it in the trash, and you along with it, and then he'd come after me."

"I know, but I'm desperate and... Don't you know someone, a doctor, who owes you a favor, and might be willing to bend the rules a little?"

"That won't work either," he said. "No one can release you, but your own doctor."

"Please, Doc. Do something. I'm begging you."

There was a moment of silence, then he said, "Where are you?"

"I'm in my damn car at the police department."

"Wait there while I make a call. Give me five minutes."

I smiled and nodded—stupid, right?—and he hung up without saying good-bye, as usual. But, true to his word, less than five minutes later he called back.

"Get yourself over to Erlanger. Doctor Napai will see you."

"Oh God! Thank you. You're a dream boat. I owe you one."

"Take it easy. Don't speed." That was all he said before hanging up.

Me? I said a quick prayer to St. Christopher, the patron saint of travelers, that if he could, would he please give me as many green lights as possible. He must have felt bad for me because I don't think I hit a single red light or even a yellow the whole way to the hospital. I made it in less than ten minutes.

Dr. Napai wasn't in the best of moods, in fact she wasn't happy at all.

"I take it you have a special friend," she said as she came into the examination room and sat down in front of me.

"You mean Doctor Sheddon? Yes, he's my friend."

"You understand that I am making an exception for you, yes?"

"I do and thank you so much. I really need to get back to work, Doctor. I'm conducting a murder investigation."

"Yes, I know. Doctor Sheddon explained the situation. I'm going against my better judgment here, Detective. But under the circumstances..." she said, slowly shining her flashlight into my eyes, one at a time. "Hmm! Hmm!" She paused again, stood back and glared at me.

"I will allow you to return to work, but I must insist that you keep your Friday appointment."

"Yes, Doctor," I replied, feeling like a naughty child.

I left the hospital with my note in my pocket and when I got to my car, I called Chief Johnston. Somehow, though, I didn't feel like I'd accomplished a whole lot. I had the uneasy feeling that I was balancing on the edge of a cliff and that at any minute someone would step up and push me over the edge.

I was starting to get another headache. Then I realized I hadn't had but one cup of coffee. That's it, I thought. Coffee. I need a booster.

"I've got your judge," Johnston said when he finally answered. "Meet me out front of the Federal Courthouse, and you'd better have a doctor's note."

It took me a little longer to get to the courthouse, and when I arrived, I couldn't find a spot and ended up parking in Harry Starke's secure lot. I didn't have time to ask permission, but I figured that after our long history together, he wouldn't mind. From there I walked the two blocks to the courthouse where the Chief was waiting for me.

The first thing he did was stick out his hand for the note. I gave it to him. He glanced at it and handed it back to me along with my gun and badge.

"Have you read it?" he asked.

"N-o... Should I have?"

"Light duties."

"Light duties?" I asked, completely confused. "What the hell does that mean?"

He smiled, something he rarely ever did, and said, "In your case, I shouldn't wonder, not a damn thing."

24

Judge Amiel Seagal was almost a midget, or should I say a little person, or just plain old short. Yeah, I know; none of them are politically correct, but what the hell, I never was that anyway. However you might describe it, though, regardless of his stature, he had a tough reputation and was a stickler for doing what's right.

I hate lawyers. They are a distraction and a disruption for just about everything I have to do, and it pains me. The only thing worse than lawyers are politicians. What was it Shakespeare said? First, kill all the lawyers, or something like that? Maybe he did, maybe he didn't. Whatever; I certainly understood the sentiment.

"Hello, my friend," Judge Seagal said to Johnston. "Take a seat, if you would." Then to me he said, "Captain. I hate that we should have to meet under such sad circumstances. My condolences to you and your team. Let me see the warrant, Wesley." He held out his hand.

"Thank you, Judge," the Chief said and handed it to him.

Seagal briefly scanned it, nodded, then signed it and handed it back. Johnston handed it on to me.

"Detective Gazzara, where'd you get that lump on your head?" the Judge asked.

Instinctively, I raised my hand to touch my head, but quickly stopped and said, "From the person named on this warrant."

He nodded, sympathetically, and said, "It's a sad truth that sometimes the bad guys win, Detective. We've all seen it. Me more than most, I think. Make sure you lock it down tight."

"Yes, sir, and thank you."

"Good luck to you, Captain."

"You can leave now, Captain," Johnston said. "I need to talk to the judge."

Oh, those heavenly words. I was so pleased that I didn't have to ride the elevator down to the lobby in close proximity to one of the most intimidating men I'd ever known. I'm talking about the Chief, of course.

I hurried out of the courthouse, down the steps, turned right and then almost ran back to my car at Harry's offices on Georgia. I didn't go inside, though I dearly would have liked to have said hello to Jacque and the guys and, yes, even Harry, but I really wasn't in the mood.

And then that decision suddenly was taken out of my hands. No sooner had my backside hit the driver's seat than Hawk called.

"I'm at Happy Henry's. Can you meet me?" he asked.

I had the engine running and my foot on the gas before I even got the words "give me ten minutes" out of my mouth.

Happy Henry's is a legend in the Tri-State area... well, in its day it was. It's called a family fun center, but I think it would be better described as a "have to see it to believe it" kind of place. I'll admit, I've been there only once in the last five years, and it was exactly the same then as it had been the first time I went with my mother when I was ten years old.

The trippy '60s-style decor could have used a coat of paint, the three mini-golf courses were in serious need of renovation, and even on a captive course such as these, you could expect to lose at least three balls per game. As for the go-carts, you can get into a worse accident colliding with someone walking than driving one of them at top speed. And the baseball batting cages... the ball machines were a relic from the past, from the Jimmy Carter era, and even when they worked, all they could produce was a slow, soft pitch.

But that's not all: the place is poorly run. Employee turnover is high. Teenagers work for half a summer before the regular employees creep them out enough for them to leave. Background checks are rarely done. Most of the staff are paid under the table in cash. Poorly maintained as the place is, though, it still manages to turn a small profit. It's one of those places everyone has to experience at least once. And it is also well-known as a spot where people getting out of rehab or jail can get work.

I parked my car and walked to the turnstile where Hawk was waiting for me. Thankfully, the place wasn't too busy.

"What have you got?" I asked.

"I talked to Pierce. He's a clown. He's never heard of Natalie, or Nate, Cassidy. He told me he leaves the everyday running of the park to his manager, a Mary Sanek. She's been here for years. I think she's the only one who has, other than Henry himself.

"I've already spoken to her," he continued, "but I couldn't get her to open up. I have a feeling they have some unsavory characters, maybe even felons or registered sex offenders working around the kids, and I spotted at least a dozen violations of the health and safety codes. I can't believe the place is allowed to stay open.

"Anyway," he continued, "I told her I wasn't interested in any of that. I just wanted some information on someone who once worked, or still works here, but she wouldn't go for it. Maybe you can get through to her. Come on, it's this way."

And Hawk led the way to a trailer-cum-office at the western edge of the park.

"It was when I mentioned Cassidy's name that she clammed up," Hawk said as we walked toward the office. "She wouldn't say another damn word, so I called you. I thought maybe another woman might—"

"Yeah, yeah, I know," I said. "Did you tell her what it was about?" Maybe it was my state of mind, the stress, or the fact that I was still grieving for Miller, I don't know, but I was angry. There's nothing more frustrating than to have someone you think might have some good information shut down and refuse to talk.

"Let's do it," I said as I pulled my hair back from my face and winced as I touched the knot under my hairline.

The trailer was probably the most modern piece of equipment in the entire park. More steel box on wheels than habitat, it was painted a sickening pee-stain yellow color and had an air conditioner sticking out of one of the only two windows on the structure. The original aluminum door had been replaced with a clunky wooden one that was about two inches too short, leaving a significant gap at the bottom. The security was a hasp and padlock. The steps were also made of wood and had seen better days; they creaked under Hawk's weight.

"Did you go inside?" I asked Hawk as he raised his hand to knock.

"No. She wouldn't invite me in. We talked out here. When she decided she didn't want to talk any more, she went inside and slammed the door."

He knocked loudly on the door and waited. He knocked again, and eventually we heard a scratchy voice from inside tell us to come in.

The inside of the trailer was even more depressing than the outside. A permanent haze of cigarette smoke clung to the ceiling, fed by a spiral of smoke that rose slowly upward from a huge ashtray full of half-smoked butts at the center of the steel desk.

Mary Sanek was seated behind the desk. She wore a dirty, crimson sweater, and her brunette hair was cut short but stood out in spikes at odd angles and looked to be in serious need of a shampoo. Her body had that classic pear shape of someone who spent most of her life seated. Her shoulders were narrow, her neck long, and her chin slanted back from her bottom lip to her neck. She reminded me of a Dr. Seuss character.

There were stacks of paper everywhere: on each side of her, piled up on a card table to her left, and on top of a row of filing cabinets to her right. The threadbare carpet, judging by the bits of crap I could see in the pale, green light of a single fluorescent tube over her head, probably hadn't seen a vacuum cleaner in under a decade. The place smelled of mold, wet dog, and stale cigarettes.

"Miss Sanek." I stepped further inside the trailer— much further than I felt comfortable with—and held up my badge. "My name is Captain Gazzara. You already know Sergeant Hawkins, I believe."

"Hello, Detective," she said, sighed, and lit another cigarette. The one she'd just stubbed out still smoldering in the ashtray.

"I'd like to talk to you about Natalie Cassidy," I said. "D'you know where she is?"

"No, I don't. Haven't seen her since Friday. Sit your-selves down," she said, waving at the three steel folding chairs in front of her desk.

I took my recorder from my pocket and asked her permission to record the interview. She rolled her eyes, coughed violently, then spluttered, "Yeah, whatever."

I spoke the usual ritual into the machine for the record, then asked her to confirm that her name was Mary Sanek.

"Oh geez," she said. "Seriously? Yeah, that's me. Look, I told Detective Hawkins here everything I know."

"That's not true," Hawk said. "You said nothing about her."

"There's nothing to tell," she replied.

"Yeah, well, I don't really buy that," I said. "Why don't you start from the beginning. When did Natalie

Cassidy start working here? Or was she calling herself Nate?"

She took a long drag off her cigarette and began to speak. Each word was accompanied by a small puff of smoke.

"*Natalie* started working here about five months ago. Well, that was this time. She'd worked here before. Last year, I think. And the year before that, maybe nine months prior." She shrugged, then continued, "We employ a lot of people. They come and go. They stay a few weeks, make a little money, go spend it, then come back again. We're one of the few places in this town that don't judge people. Henry likes to give everybody that needs it a second chance." She squinted at me as she sucked hard on the cigarette.

"What does she do here? What's her job?" I asked.

She shrugged, then said, "She does like all the others. Everybody pitches in where they can. Sometimes she'd collect the tickets in the arcade. Sometimes she'd work the mini-golf, sometimes the pettin' zoo, clean up the shit, and such. It ain't rocket science."

"How does she get along with everyone? Does she have any friends?" Hawk asked.

Mary's facial expression changed from easygoing to wary. She looked to the left, pinched her lips together, and then coughed so hard I thought she'd lose her lungs.

"Look, I don't care what people do in their personal lives—" she began.

"You're not running for office, Ms. Sanek," I said angrily. "This is a murder investigation. Political correctness is not a necessity, so please answer the question."

She glared at me, as if to say *fine, you asked for it.*

"Natalie's... different," she began. "When she first came to work, as Nate Cassidy, everyone thought that she was a dude. She was always in baggy camouflage pants and clunky boots and that hat with the panels down the sides and back. She has a deep voice, and she's strong as a frickin' ox, and she strutted around and joked with the guys about the women they'd see out there in the park. All guys do that sort of thing, don't they?" she asked, looking at Hawk.

"She sure looked and acted like a guy," she continued, "and there didn't seem to be any problems until she made her big announcement, back in 2017, I think it was."

"Which was?" I asked, already suspecting the answer.

"That her name was really Natalie, and that she was a girl, but not for much longer. No one could believe it, at first, then everyone started to say, 'yeah, now that you mention it... I should have noticed this or that,' you know."

She took another drag on her cigarette and stubbed it out.

"And you," I said, "what did you think? Were you surprised?"

"Not really, not once she come out. I was like the others: once I knew... well yeah, it made sense. Her size, for one thing. If she weighs a hundred and twenty pounds soaking wet she weighs an ounce. And she never took her shirt off like the other guys did, or wore T-shirts or those singlet undershirts, not even when it was hot outside. Always a long-sleeved flannel shirt or something similar. Then it was obvious, wasn't it? She didn't want no one to know she was taping down her breasts."

"Was she accepted after she came out?" I asked.

"Yeah, mostly, at first. Most folks around here have baggage of one sort or another. It was sort of like... Okay, so now we know you're really a girl, but that's okay. But then it became a grind, you know?"

I shook my head.

"It got to be too much, like. Everything was about her, getting her surgery and about being a guy. She bragged about the weights she could lift and how the medications her doctor had given her were working and how horny she was. She kept going on and on about how she couldn't wait until stage four or whatever to get her new parts attached."

She took another cigarette from the pack on her desk and continued, "She bragged about her time in the Marines, and that she broke her arm in basic trying to beat some record and got discharged. But I think she was full of it."

"Why do you say that?"

"My second ex-husband was a Marine. He told me if you so much as rolled your eyes at a drill instructor you'd find yourself in a world of shit. But Nate, well she insisted that she yelled at her DI on more than one occasion and had even threatened him too. But that he didn't do anything about it. Jim, my ex, said that was a load of shit; she'd never get away with it. She was constantly trying to prove how tough she was. She claimed it was because of her DI that she broke her arm, that it was his record she was going to break and he made sure she didn't."

She paused, coughed, and licked her lips. I swear her tongue was the color of a corpse. "She's full of shit," she said, shaking her head. "I don't believe a word of it."

"Did any of your employees?" I asked.

"Hell no. It got to the point where some of them would

ask her silly shit just to get her talking and see how much crap would come out of her mouth. She drank like a fish. And when she drank, she really changed. Screw the surgery. She was a regular Jekyll and Hyde."

"Did she ever turn violent?" I asked.

"Not that I saw on the premises. But I was told by some of the high school kids who worked over the summer that she tried to pick fights with some of them."

"You've got high school kids working with ex-cons?" Hawk asked.

"Are you kidding?" she asked. "Half the kids who work here have rap sheets some of the ex-cons would be proud of. You should know that detective." She sucked on her cigarette and blew out a cloud of smoke Mount Kīlauea would have been proud of.

The atmosphere inside the trailer was becoming thicker, unbearably so. I figured I was going to have to take a bath in tomato juice to get the smell out of my hair and off my skin.

"What about relationships?" I asked. "Did she have a boyfriend... girlfriend?"

"Nah. Not that I know of. She's a loner," she said. "But she liked to impress the kids. Spent most of her time with them. When they went back to school and she was left with the grown-ups, she took another turn." She tapped the cigarette with her forefinger, letting the ashes fall to the floor.

"What do you mean?" I asked.

"She was always braggin' but when the kids were gone, she started telling stories about how she's hurt some people, that she'd hurt a couple of guys and stole their wallets. She said she went into a bar and put some guy's head through a jukebox and *strolled* out of there. I'll never forget that because she said she was talking with a woman at the bar and that the woman's boyfriend had come in and gotten pissed. So, she took him down and then just *strolled* out of the place. Just *strolled*. That's what she said. No one called the cops. No one tried to stop her. That she was so badass that she could just bust up a place and walk right on out and no one could do anything about it.

"More than one of the guys told her it was all bullshit, because she wouldn't name the bar. That was when she said she killed a guy in Huntsville."

"She said that?" I asked.

"Yeah, but no one believed her. She's crazy, full of shit, a narcissist, and a regular pain in the ass. She doesn't need a dick attached; she already is one. Look, I don't care what you do. Do what you want. Pierce your damn tits, if you want, but don't come around here stirrin' up shit, okay?"

Just then Hawk's cell phone rang. "It's Robar, Cap," he said. "She's done with the shrink."

"Tell her to meet us at Cassidy's apartment. Make sure she has the location," I said. I was ready to get out of the smoky hellhole.

Hawk nodded. "I'll be outside," he said and went out of the door, leaving it wide open.

I felt the cold air rush in like an arctic blast. Unfortunately, it did little to alleviate the blanket of smoke.

I stood up, picked up my recorder, and said, "Is there anything more you can tell me that you think might help?" I asked.

"Yeah! I can tell you you're dealing with one messed-up

crazy. She thinks she's a man, for God's sake. The sad thing is, she'd be kind of pretty as a girl. I don't get it."

"Did you ever feel threatened by her?" I asked.

"Nah." She shook her head. "I don't think she has what it takes to take me on. Some of the younger people, maybe, but me? No!"

I thanked her for her time, left a business card, turned off my recorder, and asked her to call me if Cassidy turned up. Then I walked outside and took a deep breath. It was heavenly.

"Glad to be out of there, I bet," Hawk said.

"Yeah," I said feeling my head swim.

"Also, while I was waiting for you, the lab called back about that Band-Aid they found in Logan's car. They've got a profile."

"Great. Now if we could get a match... Maybe we'll find something in her apartment."

25

Natalie Cassidy lived in a large, multi-story apartment complex on the south side of town in an area it was wise to avoid, especially after dark. Hawk and I waited outside on the street until the rest of the team arrived. The team consisted of me, Hawk, Ann Robar, Mike Willis, two techs from forensics, and three uniformed cops.

We gathered at the street door, and I gave everyone a few final instructions, mainly that I was looking for physical evidence that would tie the woman to one or more of the crime scenes. This would include trophies, trace evidence—hair, fiber, fingerprints, blood, and, in particular, a pair of boots that matched the cast Hawk had retrieved from the Logan crime scene. We also needed to gather a DNA sample in order to try for a match with the blood on the Band-Aid. I knew Cassidy was my killer, but knowing's not enough to convict her; I had to prove it.

The lock on the street door—steel, painted olive green—was broken. Hawk turned the latch and we pushed on through into the lobby, an open area maybe twenty feet square with two elevators facing the door and a flight of stairs to the right of the elevators. The north wall was devoted to a bank of mailboxes, seventy-two of them in twelve layers of six; which meant, of course, that the building had twelve floors. Attached to the elevators, one on each door, were signs written in black marker on cardboard, torn from what once might have been an Amazon packing box. They stated that the elevators were "out of order." Wouldn't you know it? Cassidy's apartment was number 1105; it was on the eleventh floor.

"Oh crap," Robar said, eyeing the stairs. "Are you kidding me?"

I was in no mood for hilarity, but I couldn't help but smile at that; I knew exactly how she felt.

"Let's do it," I said, and I headed for the stairs followed by Hawk and then the rest of the team.

I swear it took the best part of ten minutes to mount those eleven flights of stairs—well, that's what it seemed like —and by the time we reached Cassidy's floor, I was all but done for. So was Robar. Hawk? What d'you think? The man is an animal. He wasn't even breathing hard.

We stood outside apartment 1105. I hoped to hell we weren't going to have to break it down; those apartment doors are made of steel for a reason, to keep people out.

No, I was hoping that Natalie was home and that she would cooperate. But that didn't seem likely. If she was willing to kill Miller, she was probably more than willing to kick up a fuss. My one concern was that we knew she was armed...

Don't get me wrong. The idea of thumping the back of

her head against the wall was more than a little intoxicating; revenge is sweet, and I needed a little sugar.

So, we stood together at the door to apartment 1105. I had an officer draw his weapon and cover the stairs in case she came upon us unawares. The other two officers stood ready with me, Robar and Hawk.

I drew my Glock, nodded to the others to do the same, then I covered the peephole with my free hand and knocked on the door with the barrel of the gun, and then we waited. No answer.

"I don't think she's home," Robar said.

"I think you're right," I said. "Damn! We're going to have to kick that steel slab in."

"Step aside, Cap. Gimme a little space," Hawk said, taking out his wallet.

I stood back, my gun trained on the door. Hawk extracted a set of picks from his wallet and set to work on the lock. It took him less than thirty seconds to open it.

It was a small studio apartment: a living room, a kitchen, and a bathroom. I switched on the light. Nothing. No electricity. The living room was empty of furniture, just a sleeping bag on the floor and a cooler with a 10-inch, battery-powered TV set on top at the foot of the sleeping bag. In one corner, there was a pile of men's clothing. I poked it gingerly with my foot, half-expecting an exodus of... hell, who knows what? Rats, maybe? I sure as hell hoped not. I hate the little bastards.

And then there were the walls. The one facing the sleeping bag was covered with photographs, all of men. Some of them were obviously models. Some were body-builders. Some were sports personalities. Many of them had cutouts of a girl's head taped over the heads of the models or bodybuilders. I assumed it was Natalie's head.

"So, this is what our girl looks like," I said, squinting; I couldn't see too well in the dim light, and I had another headache coming on. *Hey, I think I know that face...* I thought. *Where have I seen her before?* I couldn't remember; I wasn't even sure that I had seen her. *Maybe she just has one of those faces.*

I took several of the photos down and handed them to Hawk. "Go back to the office and have them copied and enlarged," I said, still staring at one of the images of her face. *I do know her... but from where?* "Then get them out to patrol. Maybe someone will spot her, though I have my doubts: she's got to know we're after her by now."

I stared again at the images on the wall. She looked like an older high school senior with a crooked smirk.

"She's over the edge... way over," Robar said, shaking her head, staring at the photographs. "She's fixated, frickin' nuts. She belongs in Moccasin Bend. Kate, we have to get this crazy bitch, and fast... But see here, this is the kind of guy she wants to be, right?" she asked, pointing to one of the altered bodybuilder images. "So why would she go after someone like Jack Logan? He didn't look anything like these guys. I doubt he did even when he was younger."

"You understated it when you said she was crazy," I said. "The woman is insane..." I stared at the images. "I don't know what to think," I said as I studied each picture in turn. There were scribbles alongside many of them, unreadable notes with arrows and circles pointing to pecs and thighs and genitals. I shook my head and went into the kitchen.

The kitchen was almost as bare as the living room. It didn't appear that Cassidy was much of a cook. Empty cereal boxes littered the counters. Empty cans that once had contained Beefaroni, Vienna Sausages, and Miller beer were piled high in the overflowing trash can. Milk cartons, fast food containers, and napkins, along with cigarette stubs in makeshift, aluminum foil ashtrays, and a whole collection of other garbage lay scattered around everywhere. It was disgusting.

From the kitchen I went to the bathroom, turned on one of the faucets, and then off again. At least she had water.

"Yikes," Robar said, as she carefully stepped into the tiny bathroom and saw the shattered mirror over the sink. "I guess she didn't like what she saw."

The bathroom was a mess. Aside from the broken mirror glass, there was a stack of mutilated porn magazines. All of the important... maybe I should call them interesting anatomical parts had either been scratched out, scribbled out, or cut out. Bits of paper lay scattered all over the floor in front of and around the commode, along with a utility knife, the blade of which was covered in blood.

"Get forensics in here," I said. "Looks like we have our DNA sample."

"Mike," I said when he entered. "We could get lucky." I pointed to the knife.

He nodded, stepped forward, lifted it carefully, and bagged it.

"And grab her toothbrush, just to be sure," I said, and as I said it, I couldn't help but wonder if maybe Cassidy had used that knife on herself. Had she harmed herself? Did she look at herself in the mirror and not like what she saw, as Ann had suggested?

"Kate? *Kate?*" Ann said, interrupting my thoughts. "Did you hear what I said?"

"I'm sorry. I was just thinking... What did you say?" My head was spinning. I was having trouble concentrating.

Robar pointed to a small leather kit that was on the corner of the toilet tank.

"I asked if you thought that might be her father's shaving kit."

I looked at it, chuckled, and then carefully picked it up. "No. It's not her dad's shaving kit. It's a hormone injection kit, if I'm not mistaken. Forensics can take it, too."

"I think we've seen enough here," I said. "We got most of what we came for. Hawk's gone to get the images copied. Now all we need is a DNA match with the Band-Aid. Maybe we'll get lucky. If so, it would make life a whole lot easier."

"I need to get out of here. I have an appointment with Doctor Harmon at two, remember?"

"Yeah," I said, still thinking, my eyes on one of the photographs. "Don't forget to drop by the department and pick up Janet."

"I hadn't forgotten. What are you going to do now, Cap?"

I looked at my watch and squinted. It was just after one o'clock in the afternoon, and my head was really beginning to bother me. *What the hell's wrong with me?* And then I realized I'd still had only one cup of coffee since I left home that morning, and none since before Happy Henry, or had I? Damned if I could remember. *So no coffee, then?* No wonder I felt like hell; coffee to a cop is like gasoline to a car. I needed a fill-up.

"I'm going to go get something to eat," I replied to Ann, "then back to the office. I'll see you both there when you get done with the doctor. Mike, you'll be a while, right?"

He nodded. I told the uniforms to remain stationed at the door and the stairwell to protect Mike and his team, and I left the building.

26

A s I drove back to the office, I stopped by a Five Guys restaurant and grabbed a burger with everything, a sack of French fries, and a quart of black coffee, all to go—yes, I know, the calories, but what the hell. I spend too much time on my feet for them to matter a whole lot. And, with what I was dealing with, I had no doubt my body could handle the extra intake with ease.

And so I drove, and as I drove, I munched and I drank, but most of all I wondered where on God's green earth Natalie-Nate Cassidy could be hiding; she had to be somewhere in the city.

I thought about the cutouts on the apartment wall. It was obvious she had some sort of love-hate relationship with herself, that her dream was to be like the muscular, chiseled men in the images, which is why she'd taped her own head to many of them. But why was she targeting older, harmless guys who didn't look anything like them, or her dream? Was it a power thing? Domination? And did she or did she not have an accomplice? If she did, who the hell was it? If she didn't, what was behind the shots in the back of the head?

Then it dawned on me.

"That's why!" I said to the steering wheel. "These guys, her victims, would never hit a girl; they couldn't or wouldn't fight back. A jock, a bodybuilder on steroids, or even a younger guy could easily backhand her into the middle of next week." *Especially if she was prancing around like a dude with a smart mouth and a chip on his shoulder,* I thought. *Hmm. Jack Logan was the kind of guy who liked his sports and maybe a beer or two, but then he went home to his wife every night, lived a plain and simple life. And he was overweight and about as fit as a Bundt cake. He wasn't a threat to anyone. Neither was Miller, for Pete's sake.*

The thought made me angry. She didn't know Lennie Miller was just a nice young man with a penchant for all things technical. A guy who thought a gun was too dangerous to touch, let alone carry, even though his job required it. Janet was smaller than her, but not much, so she was an easy target. With Robar, Natalie was smart and didn't confront her directly. So instead, she vandalized her car. But what was it about Miller that made her think he was the easy mark?

And then I realized two things. One: it wasn't my people that were the actual targets. It was me. By attacking them, she was attacking me, the one person who could and would bring her down. Two: I realized where I'd seen her before. She was the woman I'd met talking to my neighbor outside my apartment: the bitch was checking me out.

"I'll kill the frickin' bitch," I snarled to myself as I banged my wrists on the steering wheel. And suddenly I was in big trouble. I was sweaty and cold, and my stomach was flipping. I had to pull over at an auto parts store and before I knew it, I was outside my car at the rear bumper saying goodbye to the burger, fries, and coffee. *Damn it all to hell.*

"Hey, are you okay?"

It was a guy in a red company polo shirt; he obviously worked at the store. And I could see another, inside, watching me through the plate glass window with interest, a snide smirk on his face.

"I'll be fine, but thanks," I said, gulping at the air and spitting the final remnants of a fourteen-dollar meal onto the ground. "I'm sorry about the mess." I held my stomach and my head swam for several seconds before I could focus and stand up straight.

"Don't worry about it," he said. "I'll hose it away. You look like shit. D'you want me to call someone for you?" He looked genuinely worried.

"Geez, thanks for the compliment." I managed a small smile, then said, "No, but thanks. I'll be fine. Again, I'm sorry."

He nodded and went back inside. The guy in the window was still grinning at me. I was tempted to give him the middle finger, but I didn't. Instead, I climbed in back behind the wheel, started the engine, and drove away.

Ten minutes later I pulled into the parking lot at the rear of the police department, fully recovered from my embarrassing encounter at the auto parts store, but still feeling like crap and in need of a shower, which is what I did. I went to the locker room, stripped off my clothes, and washed away my blues: mood, that is, not my uniform. I was wearing plain clothes, remember?

Like the proverbial Boy Scout, I was always prepared, and thus I kept a couple of spare pairs of jeans, several sets of clean underwear, and a couple of clean tops in my locker. That being so, when I emerged from the locker room, I felt like a princess and ready for just about anything. Unfortunately, I still looked like hell.

The feeling of euphoria? It didn't last for more than a few minutes... just until I walked into the situation room and saw Miller's empty desk.

I stood for a second, staring at it, looking at it, but not seeing it, if you know what I mean. And then I realized that it was only a matter of time before someone else would be sitting there, and I felt my eyes begin to water. I turned away. I couldn't let it happen; I could cry, but not in the situation room.

I hurried to my office and closed the door, happy to be able to shut out the rest of the world, at least for a few minutes, but still I choked it back. And then my phone rang.

"Gazzara," I muttered, barely loud enough for me to hear, let alone the caller.

"Good afternoon, Captain. This is Chief Gunnery Sergeant Wilcox Dorman of the United States Marine Corps over here in Columbus, Georgia. I hope I'm not disturbing you."

Who? What? I don't know any...

"Good afternoon, Gunnery Sergeant. This is a surprise. What can I do for you?"

"Well, I think it's more what I can do for you. I understand that you've had the unfortunate luck of meeting Miss Natalie Cassidy."

He had a nice voice and spoke as if he was giving orders. I liked the sound of him.

"Not yet, not to speak to I haven't, but I'm working on it and hope to meet her *very* soon. And you know this... how?"

"Let's just say a little bird told me. The truth is that with an Entry Level Separation like hers, we try to keep an eye on them, at least for a while, to make sure they get properly acclimated to civilian life again... or, as in this particular case, not."

"Yes, not, and that's putting it mildly, Gunny. So, what is it you can do for me? Would it be breaking the rules if you told me the reason for her separation?"

"It would, but in this case, I'll tell you. Miss Cassidy had it in her pretty little head that joining the Marine Corps would be the perfect way to get the government to pay for her gender reassignment surgery. When she found out that it wasn't going to be quite that easy, and that she would be required to complete the six-year active status commitment she signed up for... well, it was a deal-breaker for her. In a nutshell, she went nuts. Hers was a psychological separation."

I sat there for a moment, unsure of what to say next. Fortunately, I didn't have to.

"Miss Cassidy had no intention of serving out her term," he continued. "She was convinced that Uncle Sam would pay for her change of gender, and then she'd be on her merry way to go bone Miss Teen USA. Pardon my language."

"No apology necessary, Gunny. I've said far worse

myself over these past couple of weeks... Look, I shouldn't be talking to you about it over the phone. In fact, I'm under strict orders from my chief of police to keep what I know under wraps until I can make an arrest, but I will tell you this: she's responsible for the death of a member of my team."

I don't know why I spilled my guts like that to him. Maybe it was the sound of his voice. Maybe I felt that somehow I could trust him, or maybe it was just because at that moment I needed to talk to someone who understood how I was feeling. Whatever! The words just spilled out, and suddenly I felt like someone had sucked the poison from my wound.

"I am sorry, Detective. May I offer you my condolences?" So he did understand. "So, she's not in custody?"

"Unfortunately, no. But we're closing in," I lied. I didn't want to sound completely incompetent.

"Well, I am glad to hear that, but the reason for my call was because I thought you might like to know that when Cassidy was with us, she corresponded often with a friend by the name of Tilly Montgomery. She was listed as Cassidy's emergency contact, the only one, in fact. Montgomery lives in Chattanooga."

Oh... m'God! Are you serious? Oh Lordy, I think I'm in love.

"Gunny, if you ever find yourself in the Chattanooga area, I'd like to buy you a drink. Now, if you wouldn't mind, please give me that address."

27

I t didn't take me long to grab Robar and for her to drive me to Tilly Montgomery's home. *Light duties, my ass.*

Her house on the north side of the river looked like it hadn't seen an update since its construction in the early sixties. It was tiny, situated on a tired, worn-out street and looked like it had barely enough room for one person to live there, let alone a couple. But that wasn't the worst part; there were cats, hundreds of 'em—okay, so there were eight —lying and roaming around the front porch, and that made me afraid of what we might encounter on the inside. I am *not* a cat person.

"A crazy cat lady?" Robar asked and, evidently, from her tone, she wasn't a cat person either.

"Looks that way," I said as I knocked on the front door. "You want to go check round back?"

She nodded and left.

"Who ith it? Who'th out there?" the voice lisped.

"Someone doesn't have her dentures in yet," I muttered.

"Miss Tilly Montgomery?" I asked and then identified myself.

"I'd like to talk to—"

"Who did you thay you are?"

"My name is Detective Gazzara," I repeated. "I'm here to talk to you about Natalie Cassidy."

One of the dirty lace curtains that hung across the window in the front door moved to one side, and the woman peeked through at me. She wasn't as old as I'd expected from the sound of her voice. She was maybe in her late fifties; her weather-worn skin made her look older.

"Nate isn't here," Tilly Montgomery said through the closed door, frowning.

"I didn't ask if she was," I said firmly. "I said I want to talk to you. Please open the door."

The curtain dropped back into place. I listened and watched. I could see the woman through the curtain. She seemed to be talking to herself, mumbling. I couldn't make out what she was saying or who she was talking to, but after what I'd just been through, I was taking no more chances. I drew my weapon and held it down by my thigh, ready.

Finally, after a couple clicks and the swipe of a security chain, the door opened and... "Oh geez," I muttered as the wave of ammonia from an overabundance of cat litter wafted through the opening, almost overwhelming me.

Mary Sanek's trailer was a palace compared to this place. I took a step back and took a deep breath.

"Nate isn't here," she said. "I haven't seen him in months. You'd better come on in then." And she shuffled backward, pulling the door open to make room for me to step inside.

It was dark inside, gloomy, and the woman was obviously a hoarder. It was like something out of an old movie. I was unnerved, but not by the atmosphere; by more than twenty pairs of golden eyes that stared at me, unblinking. *Holy cow!*

"Mrs. Montgomery—"

"Call me Tilly," she said as she waved for me to follow her into the kitchen. I heard a knock at the back door and saw Robar's silhouette through the door window.

I looked around. It appeared that Montgomery lived alone in the small house... with her cats.

I holstered my weapon. She didn't seem to notice. The back door was secured by two large bolts, a chain, and a lock. Ann knocked again.

"Who's that out back?" Montgomery asked, making sure I was between her and the door.

"It's just my partner, Detective Robar. Is it all right if I let her in?"

She nodded and I drew back the bolts, undid the chain, turned the key in the lock, and opened the door for Ann to step inside.

"This is Detective Robar," I said as Ann flashed her ID. "I'm sorry to bother you, Ms. Montgomery—"

"I told you to call me Tilly," she said, interrupting me.

"Tilly, yes. As I was saying, Tilly, we're worried about Natalie. She's in a lot of trouble. D'you have any idea where she might be?"

"No. I told you. I haven't seen her in... three months, it must be."

"What is your relationship to Natalie?"

"It's not Natalie. It's Nate now, ain't it?" she asked, plonking herself down at the kitchen table.

Ann sat down across from her. I remained standing. I had no idea what might be on those seats... I don't like cats.

"Didn't he get all his stuff done like he said?" Tilly asked.

She was looking at me as if I might be the bearer of the big news she'd been waiting for.

"What stuff are you talking about?" Ann asked.

"His surgery, of course. The last time I talked to him, he said he almost had enough money to get his new bits attached, you know." She wrinkled her face and pointed down at her crotch.

I actually shuddered.

"No. She hasn't had the surgery yet," I replied. "How well do you know her?" I asked, finding the whole situation weird.

"I've known *him* since *he* was a kid. I'd say that I met him when he was about thirteen years old. Maybe fourteen. I'm the one who helped him, you know," Tilly said as she looked me squarely in the face. She was wearing a housecoat with sweatpants underneath and a thin necklace made of seed beads around her neck. Her hair was a patchwork of gray and mousy brown cut into a bob style.

I looked around the room. The sink was filled with dishes, the counter cluttered with coupons and junk mail flyers and cans of pork and beans, corn, carrots, Dinty Moore stew and half a loaf of bread.

"What did you help him with?" I asked, taking out my recorder and turning it on.

She looked at the little machine as I set it down in front of her.

"It's just so I don't forget what we talk about," I said. "D'you mind?"

She glared at it, then at me, then at Ann, then at the recorder again. Finally, she shrugged and nodded.

"I suppose it will be okay," she said, still staring at the machine. "Nate was wrong from the get-go. He was born in the wrong body; he wasn't meant to be in that body at all. He was a strong young man inside a weak body, he was. I could see it all along. I just knew it. I told him so."

My heart began to race.

"Are you trying to tell me that you convinced a young girl that she was really a boy?"

"I didn't have to convince him. He knew it, just like I did. I just offered him my support. I didn't judge him. Like I can tell you're doing right now." She raised her chin and looked defiantly down her nose at me.

"You've got to forgive me, Tilly. It isn't every day I hear someone claim responsibility for persuading someone to reject their gender. Why would you do that?" I looked down at Robar. She looked as bumfuzzled as I was.

"He wasn't happy, you see. He wanted to be a boy, a man. Strong. He hated wearing dresses and heels and bras and panties and all. When I let him wear my late husband's shirts and pants, he was a different person, happy, like. You know, you could just see how much better he felt. Even after all these years, I can still see it as clear as day. He looked so much like my Albert." She smirked up at me.

And there it was. I'm no shrink, but I knew instantly what had happened. This stupid woman had tried to replace her dead husband with a vulnerable young girl and had turned her into a serial killer. The old bitch was as responsible for those deaths as was Natalie.

I stood for a moment trying to figure out what to say next, then Ann stepped in.

"When Nate came back to see you, did he say anything about where he'd been or what he had been doing?" she asked.

"The last time I spoke to him, he left rather quickly."

"Why is that?" Ann asked.

"I don't know... You know how men are. They're always nice to you when they want something, but when you want something in return... well, they are not so nice then, are they? They're not giving creatures, not like my pussy cats," she said, a tight smile on her lips.

I say smile, but it was more half sneer and half smirk, as if she'd at last noticed the smell in her own house. Her lips pinched into a pout, and she wrinkled her nose. And then I got it, and I almost puked. I looked at Robar. She'd gotten it too; at least I thought she had. Together we stared at the woman, disbelieving what we were thinking... well, *I* was.

"And what was it you wanted in return from him?" Robar asked, and I could tell she was dreading the answer.

Tilly licked her lips and pinched her eyebrows together. "After all the years I helped him, nurtured him, accepted him. Well, he was coming along nicely, becoming more muscular... you know, and I knew he had feelings for me."

"Were you and Nate in a sexual relationship?" I asked while attempting to stay calm, stoic.

"Oh no. We never had sex," Tilly said, looking first at me than at Robar. "No, we never had sex."

"Were you intimate in other ways?" Ann asked.

She looked away, avoided the question, and said, "Look, like I said, I haven't seen Nate in nearly three months. I doubt I'll see him any time soon."

"So you *were* intimate with him?" Ann persisted.

"Intimate? What does that mean? I told you already. We didn't have sex."

And then I remembered the words I'd heard so many times over the years on TV. "I... never... had... sex... with that woman."

I shook my head and turned away. I needed a break from the old woman, so I wandered out of the kitchen, into the living room.

"Where's she going?" I heard her say.

"She'll be back. Now please, answer the question," I heard Ann say, then I shut the rest of it out and concentrated on the living room; big mistake.

First, I came under the stare of all those eyes. Second, there was no place to sit that wasn't covered in newspapers or cat hair. The television was on with the volume turned down. Third, the most repulsive thing I think I ever encountered was the huge, pink vibrator on the table next to the recliner. *Oh... m'God! Are you kidding me? That's freakin' disgusting.* I swear, I've seen horses less well-endowed. I backed out of the room, turned, and went back into the kitchen, the image of the giant dildo stamped indelibly on my psyche.

"Did you know," I said, "that you were the only person listed in her military file as her next-of-kin? You must have meant something to her. And if you did, mean something to her, don't you think there's a chance she might come back?"

Tilly's eyes lit up for the first time since we arrived. She reminded me of one of her cats, waiting beside a hole in the baseboard, knowing there was a mouse inside, and that it had to come out sooner or later.

"Him," she said. "You mean him. She's a him."

"Yes, I meant to say him. I'm sorry, Tilly," I lied. "So, if Nate does come back, will you call me? He's in trouble, Tilly. Big trouble. He needs help. And if you try to hide him, spare him from taking responsibility, you could find yourself in trouble too," I said plainly, watching the fire in her eyes fade and finally die.

She looked at me suspiciously.

I continued, "The truth will have to come out, Tilly. All of it. It always does."

I set my card down on the table and picked up my recorder. Tilly looked at the card as if it had legs and might scurry at her any second. She looked up at me, then at Ann, but she said nothing. I turned off the recorder and we left her sitting there, alone with her thoughts... and I shuddered to think what they might have been.

"Oh, my God," Ann said as she opened the driver's side door and got in. "I need to go to the fire department and have 'em put me through the hazmat unit. What the hell *was* that?" she asked, shimmying her shoulders with the willies. "Just when I think I've seen humanity at its lowest, someone manages to shove it down a couple more notches."

"She was... I'm at a loss for words," I said, and I was, truly.

I sat beside Ann for a moment. She pushed the starter button and eased the car away from the curb, made a U-turn, and headed back in the direction of Amnicola Highway.

"Find us a coffee shop," I said. "I need to wash my mouth out."

She pulled into the drive-through at Starbucks at Hamilton Place and ordered two large black coffees. Two minutes later we were back on 153 heading toward the police department.

I decided I didn't want to be the only one that had had fun at Tilly Montgomery's home, so I told Ann about the dildo.

"Holy shit!" she said. "Why did you do that? I didn't need to know that. D'you have any idea what's going on inside my head? It's disgusting. You really do need to wash your mouth out."

And for the first time in days, I was able to sit back and relax, and even smile, just a little. But, at the back of my mind, I couldn't help feeling that Tilly Montgomery was more than partially responsible for the way Natalie Cassidy had turned into a monster.

Ann pulled into the parking lot at the rear of the PD, shut off the engine and said, "It's almost five. If it's okay with you, I think I'm going to call it a day, Kate. That was just too much to handle. Wait until I tell Hawk about it."

"Yes, sure. Go on home to the kids. Relax. We can talk to Hawk in the morning. You and him... you get along well, right? I think he likes you, Ann."

"Ha! Don't even go there, Kate. Hawk and I are just friends. I can talk to him like I can talk to no one else. You name it, he's been there, done that. He understands." She smiled, then continued, "You know how hard it is to find someone to talk to about this stuff. Could you imagine talking to say... oh, I don't know, my husband, about Tilly Montgomery? He'd cringe and tell me for the umpty-eleventh time that I shouldn't be in this line of work, or that there's something radically wrong with me. And Lord knows, he might even be right."

"Yes," I said. "You're right about that." And suddenly, for no reason I could think of, I remembered my conversation with Gunnery Sergeant Wilcox Dorman, and I wondered what it would be like to talk to him about Tilly Montgomery, sans the dildo, of course. I smiled at the thought and made a mental note to call him when the case was over, or not.

What was I even doing thinking about it? One thing I *was* sure of was that I stunk from the cat house... *Yeah,* I thought. *That's what it was, a freakin' cat house.*

My head was aching again. It wasn't bad, but it was there, lurking under the surface and just didn't seem to want to go away. *Maybe it's because I'm hungry,* I thought, as I sipped my coffee.

I tried to think of something I could eat that might hit the spot, that would stay down, or wouldn't take too long in the oven. *Not a burger, that's for sure, nor a frickin' pizza!* In fact, the idea of eating anything at all made my stomach turn. *Maybe some chicken broth and crackers. That might do the trick.*

"Did you hear what I said, Kate?" Robar said, interrupting my thoughts.

"I'm sorry. What?"

"I said we need to take up a collection for Lennie's

family to help pay his funeral costs. We should help his mother do Lennie right."

"Of course. Count me in," I said, climbing out of the car. "I'm going on home. I'll see you tomorrow."

It was a pleasant afternoon. The rain had stopped, finally, and the sky, already dark, was clear. The roads were also clear, which was unusual for a Monday. I was looking forward to a quiet evening, another shower, my sweats, and a good night's sleep. Yeah, that's what I was thinking, and I couldn't have been more wrong.

28

It was just after five-thirty when I got home that evening. I went straight to the bedroom, slipped out of my clothes and then into the shower. I left the bathroom light off and showered by the soft glow from the lamp on my bedside table. After dumping half a bottle of my lavender shampoo on my head and rubbing myself down from head to toe, I felt that maybe I'd managed to scrub the smell of cat litter from my skin and out of my hair.

I toweled off, wrapped the towel around me, went into the living room, sat down on the couch, and began to think back over the events of the past several days. It was a circus. There were more weird twists and turns than I could count, and I still had no physical evidence that Natalie Cassidy had killed anyone, not even Lennie Miller. I knew it; deep down I knew it, but that wasn't enough.

"Why him?" I whispered. The sound of my own voice set off an alarm in my head and I winced. "How in the world did she know about us? That we were onto her? The only one who hadn't been attacked was Hawk. Why?"

Then I thought of all those pictures in Natalie's apartment, and I knew why. Hawk was more than she could handle.

I went to my bedroom. It was cool and dark, and I was sure that once my body relaxed on the soft mattress, my head cradled on a pillow, I'd soon fall asleep. But I didn't. I was wired. It was as if someone had hooked me up to an IV of liquid caffeine. My eyes popped open; my mind raced from one uncomfortable topic to another: Lennie, Hawk, the gunnery sergeant, the cold cases on my desk, Janet lying in the hospital, the images on Cassidy's wall, the images on the whiteboard in the office, Lennie, that annoying TV blurb for my insurance company I'd heard a million times and kept barging into my thoughts like a child screaming for candy in WalMart, the giant dildo, Ann... Lennie, that damned great dildo... *Geez!* I couldn't focus on anything. I couldn't keep a single real thought in my head for more than a couple seconds. I was experiencing bouts of dizziness, my body ached and wanted to rest, but it was impossible.

I sat up and went to the kitchen and grabbed a new bottle of red wine from the fridge. I uncorked it, grabbed the aspirin bottle, opened it, shook two of the little tablets into my hand, and washed them down with a single huge gulp of wine. *That should do the trick.* I was sure of it.

I sat down on the couch, waited for a minute, then swung my legs up, laid my head back on the armrest and... Thankfully, I dozed off. Unfortunately not for long, not more than thirty minutes, and it wasn't the deep sleep I needed, and I was still aware of where I was and that I couldn't sleep.

Finally, I gave it up. I opened my eyes feeling like I'd

3

5

just spent five hours in hell, and I suppose, on thinking back, that was precisely where I'd been.

I decided it was time I faced the fact that I wasn't going to get any real sleep that night. I thought about going for a run, but that idea brought on an attack of the jitters. That bitch could be out there somewhere waiting for me.

I thought of reaching out to Janet or Ann but quickly backed away from that idea. I was their Captain. They could come to me, but I couldn't go to either of them. I even thought about calling Harry Starke, but quickly gave up on that idea.

I paced the floor. I tried to watch television. Reading was out of the question, and doing any kind of work that required I stare at a computer screen also didn't appeal to me. I straightened up the kitchen. I put on the radio and listened to some talk show but just got more aggravated. When I looked at the clock, I was shocked to see that it wasn't even ten o'clock yet; I had the whole damn night ahead of me... and I freaked. I was frickin' desperate... and then I had a thought.

With my brain feeling like cotton candy, I went to my bedroom and sorted through my purse and found Dr. Joon Napai's business card. I'd remembered she'd written her personal cell phone number on the back of it, in case of an emergency. Well, this was it; this was an emergency. She answered almost immediately, bless her. Her voice, the Indian accent, was soothing, calming, and I asked her for help.

"If I can," she said. "Please tell me, how have you been feeling?"

"My mind's a mess. I can't sleep. I can't seem to focus on anything. Oh, I'm okay. I'm not in any kind of trouble, or danger, or, whatever but, like I said, I can't sleep... and I'm dog tired. I have to sleep, Doctor. I took some aspirin, but they didn't help."

"Aside from not being able to focus," she said, "have there been any other symptoms that you've noticed that are out of the ordinary?"

"Well... I haven't had much of an appetite. I've been a bit dizzy, at times. The thought of eating makes me feel like I want to vomit."

"Detective, you sound like you are under a lot of stress. "Can you drive? If not, call an Uber and come and see me. I'm at the hospital."

"Oh geez, thank you. I'll be there as soon as I can."

"And breathe, Captain, breathe deeply. It will help."

"That wasn't so hard now, was it, Kate?" I asked myself as I slipped into a clean sweat suit, a navy blue one with a Civil War-era cannon on the front along with the numbers 186 stamped in yellow over the right breast and over the right hip bone. I put my tennis shoes on and tied my hair up in a ponytail. Then I grabbed my purse and headed downstairs, out through the front door and onto the steps where I paused to do some deep breathing, as Dr. Joon had instructed. It was at that moment I was overcome by a terrible feeling of impending doom. I swear I felt the hair on the back of my neck stand up.

"Don't say a word, bitch," a voice to my right said, "or I'll shoot you right where you are."

I turned and looked toward the end of my building and,

just a few yards away, almost hidden in the shadows at the corner, I could just make out the shape of a person pointing a gun at me. I couldn't see her face, but I knew instantly who it was.

"Just walk to your car," Cassidy said, gesturing with the pistol. "Don't do anything stupid."

Reluctantly, I did as I was told.

"Stand still. Reach behind you and hand over the keys. Don't look, just keep facing forward. Good, now get into the car... on the driver's side... That's it. Easy now. Slide over into the other seat. Just remember I have my gun on you, and I won't hesitate. I killed your partner right here, and I'm not afraid to kill you, too."

I did exactly as she said. She waited until I was in the passenger seat, then, without taking her eyes off me, carefully, slowly climbed into the driver's seat, keeping the gun trained on me, her hand steady as a rock.

Now I knew how Jack Logan, Cappy Mallard, and the others had gotten into their seats, and I also knew how they must have felt.

Me? I felt strangely calm. I knew I was about to face the final conflict, maybe my own personal end of days. Was I ready for it? No, but I knew deep down that I would rise to the occasion; I always did. She had the advantage, but I was a smartass and knew exactly how to take it away from her... at least I thought I did.

When she got into the car, slammed the door shut and pressed the lock button, I turned sideways in my seat and stared at her. She was wearing the same camouflage pants, the same baggy shirt, the same stupid hat with the flaps. I thought it was stupid that night I first saw her—him—in the incident room, sitting in the seat next to Robar's desk, complaining about his ex-girlfriend assaulting him.

"You really need to change your look," I said, casually. "You're dressed exactly the same as when you came to the PD to piss on your girlfriend."

"Ex-girlfriend, and I like the way I look."

"Brown, you said your name was, as I recall. Good choice, Natalie. You look like shit." The headache was gone. I felt good. I was in my element. I had no fear of this strange little man-woman that was holding me at gunpoint. I doubted very much that she was planning to kill me, but what was she planning?

"I'm not Natalie anymore," she said. Her voice was deep for a female but not overly masculine either. "I haven't been for a long time. My name is Nate. Now, you and I are going for a drive."

And so I sat there, in the passenger seat, a hostage in my own car, and I cursed my stupidity. There was little I could do but sit still and wait for something to break, or not. The only plan I had was to try to piss the woman off to the point where she would lose it and maybe make a mistake. It wasn't much, but it was all I could come up with. One thing I was sure of, though, was that things were coming to a head; it was almost over. No matter that I was a hostage, I had her. She'd either have to kill me or I'd put her away for good.

If she killed me, it would only be a matter of time before Hawk and Ann took her down.

"You know," she said, still driving with one hand, the

other holding the gun almost at my head. "I saw you that day, after I'd killed that fat guy, Jack. I was in the field, just a few rows down. You guys," she shook her head. "Pathetic. You didn't even conduct a proper search of the area," she taunted.

I clenched my fists and wondered if I could smack the gun out of her hand. Without turning my head, I glanced sideways. She had her finger on the trigger. *Too risky!*

"I knew who you were, big shot," she rambled on. "You've been in the news a lot lately. So I thought I'd check y'all out. See what you were doing to catch me."

She waited for me to answer. I didn't.

"Cat got your tongue, miss fancy detective?" Natalie chuckled. "I have to admit, I was impressed, but that Detective Robar... The silly bitch actually told me what car she was driving. You know, I hated to slash the tires on that sweet ride, but she gave up the information without even being asked, like she was daring me to do something to it."

"You're delusional, Natalie. That wasn't what she was doing. She was just making conversation. You don't impress me."

"I told you, my name is Nate."

"Sure it is. And believe it or not, I understand how you feel. You were born in the wrong body. You identify as a male. I can buy that. But the killing? What good does that do?" I hissed. "When did ambushing good, decent guys who never hurt anyone... when did that become a guy thing?"

"Are you kidding?" she asked. "It's always been about that. I've always known that I'm really a male. Men are strong. They have muscles. They fight and hunt and kill and screw. That's it. It's the natural order of things, always has been, ever since Abel killed Cain. It's called the survival of the fittest. Guys are born to kill... and that guy at The Sovereign? He was just like all the others: fat, weak, stupid. He wasn't a man."

"It's Cain that killed Abel, dumbass. His name was Jack Logan, by the way," I snapped. "And he was someone's husband."

"Abel Dumbass? Hahaha, that's just too funny... He was a disgusting blob." The laughter turned to a snarl. "One too many chili dogs and supersized Mountain Dews made him soft, slow, and ignorant. You should have seen what he was eating. It was frickin' disgusting," she said, and she actually shuddered.

"He was kind to you," I said. "He didn't come onto you or assault you. You killed him just for the hell of it. You really are certifiable. You're nothing. Just a silly little girl playing dress up and killing for the fun of it. But you're not going to get away with it, Natalie."

"It's Nate! Bitch!" she shouted at me. "And you know nothing about me. Yeah, I'm gettin' away with it, and you're in no position to do a damn thing about it."

She was right there. I didn't have the upper hand at all. She held all the cards.

"I killed him because he was a fat slug, the same reason I offed your fat friend with the blond hair."

My stomach tightened; she was talking about Lennie. I didn't answer; I couldn't.

Her eyes constantly darted back and forth as she drove, from the road to me and back again. Never for a second did the gun waver, and never once did she give me an opportunity to make a move. *Geez, I would have thought her arm would have been getting tired by now.*

"I guess the so-called mandatory fitness guidelines for the police department are just a suggestion." She laughed again, giggled. "He looked like he was well on his way to being a fat-ass desk jockey, too fat to chase anyone down on the street. Unless they were carrying a greasy sack of Krystal's or something and he was hungry."

"You piece of shit," I snarled. "You know nothing about him. He was a good man."

"Right. Sure he was."

I watched her knuckles whiten as she squeezed the grip of the gun.

"See," she continued, "there are two kinds of men in this world. There are men who see life as just a day-by-day occurrence. And then there are men like me who grab onto life and make it their own."

I snorted and turned my head to look at her. "That's just frickin' dumb," I said. "Even if it made any sense, it wouldn't matter because you're neither one. You're neither woman nor man. As I said, you're just a silly little girl with delusions of... not grandeur, that's for sure. Look at you, even your coat's too big for you."

"Shut up!" she screamed.

Her voice had taken on a wild edge, and I knew we were getting closer and closer to that point of no return. I also knew that whatever the outcome of the next several minutes, it wasn't going to end well. Natalie Cassidy was a killer, and a cop killer to boot, but she was also transgender. She'd become the media's favorite victim, and my name would be shit. But at that moment, I couldn't worry about that. I had to keep the crazy bitch off balance, if I could; if she was flustered and upset, I figured she'd eventually screw up, and I'd get my chance.

"What? You thought you were something special, right? But now you're just confused," I said, chuckling.

"Me confused?" she said, calmer now. "Not hardly. Tell me something. What did your boss say when he told you I'd filed a complaint against you? I'll bet he was pissed that his superstar had screwed up." She laughed, but not as hard as I did.

"Are you kiddin' me?" I asked, laughing at her. "D'you think for one minute that you fooled anybody? If you did, you're a frickin' idiot, as well as a confused little girl."

"Stop calling me that," she yelled. "I'll shoot you in the head; I swear I will."

"You're not going to shoot me," I said, with a whole lot more confidence than I actually felt. "You don't have the balls to look me in the..." And then I really laughed. "You don't have the balls... Ha ha ha. Oh, that's funny. You really don't have the balls, do you?"

"You freakin' dyke," she howled.

"Not me, Natalie. You're the dy—"

And then she hit me, sideswiped me in the mouth with the barrel of the gun. I swear I felt my teeth move, and the pain... Geez, my entire body froze. I felt the warm blood drip from the side of my lip down my chin and the bitter taste of copper in my mouth.

"My name is Nate, you bitch! And if you don't stop calling me Natalie, I'll kill you right now and dump your body where they'll never find it!" She was becoming hysterical.

"I know what you're trying to do!" she yelled. "You're trying to piss me off, so I'll make a mistake. Well you can forget it. I'm gonna put a bullet through your pathetic little brain. You're gonna make me famous."

"Famous?" I ran my tongue along my teeth. They were all still intact. I put my hand to my mouth. My lip was split, top and bottom, and blood was dripping from my chin. "Why don't you put that thing down and stop the car and step outside? I'll make you famous. I'll beat your silly little girly face to a pulp."

"You don't have what it takes," she muttered, more to herself than to me, and then she continued, muttering, shaking her head, "You have no idea what my end game is. I joined the military. They were supposed to help me get my surgery. But they expected—"

"They expected you to serve out your contract," I said and braced myself for another crack on the head. It didn't come. And then I became aware of where it was we were going. We'd just turned onto Rural Road 18, and I realized I had to do something quick or I was going to end up like Jack Logan.

"They expected me to wait six more years," she mumbled. "How could I serve with my body like this? It was all their fault." And then she began to curse and swear, calling everyone in the United States Marine Corps, including Gunny Dorman, the vilest names I'd ever heard, and I've heard some.

"If that was all you wanted, why didn't you just save your money and pay for the surgery yourself? Why did you have to kill all those people? It wasn't their fault you're what you are. They didn't do anything to you."

"You'll never understand," she said as she hit the gas and we tore off down RR18 in the direction of Jack Logan's demise. Her face had changed, softened. Her eyes looked blank. She was in another world.

"D'you think this is what I wanted to be? D'you think I chose to be like this? I could have been okay with it, you know? Being a girl. I could have been okay; really I could. But it was all wrong, see? She told me I was all wrong and that only I could fix it," she stuttered.

Had my face not been hurting, I might have almost felt sorry for her. I had a feeling the girl inside was trying to come out. And then I got it. She wasn't a transgender at all; she was suffering from multiple personality disorder. And Nate was the dominant entity, and I knew who was responsible for it: Tilly Freakin' Montgomery.

"Natalie," I said carefully. "I saw Tilly Montgomery today. Did she hurt you?"

"No! She helped me! She's the only one who ever did."

"Your father is still alive, you know," I said. "Why didn't you ever go to him? Why didn't you ask him for help?" I was stalling. There was no telling when she was going to pull over and put me out of my misery.

"I couldn't... He's wonderful... I couldn't let him see what I'd become." Those were probably the first honest words the woman had uttered in a long time.

"Put the gun down, Natalie," I said as she squeezed the steering wheel until the knuckles of her left hand were white. She was beginning to feel the strain in her right arm; her hand was trembling.

Holy crap, I thought. *I hope that thing doesn't have a hair trigger*.

"We can talk it through," I said gently. "We can straighten this mess out, Natalie, if you'll just put the gun down and talk to me for—"

"I warned you not to call me that name," she screamed.

29

The car, speeding now, was almost out of control. She was driving so fast everything was a blur. The moon was a silver disc, the sky a field of stars. It was a beautiful night, but I saw it only in short glimpses as the car careened onward. My mouth was dry, my lips and teeth hurt like hell, and there was nothing going on between my ears. It was as if my brain had quit working. I tried to shake it off but couldn't, and all the while Natalie was muttering to herself as she drove, saying vile and hateful things about women and girls and me... and even Janet.

"You people," she said. "You have your badges and your guns and all sorts of other shit, but you're nothing. You don't know how to use any of it. You're so easily manipulated, clueless, stupid, weak... *women*." She spit out the last word as if it was something foul, which to her, I suppose it was.

"Tell me," she said. "The cute one; the redhead who looks like a schoolgirl; is she still in the hospital? I felt sorry for her. I really hated to leave her there on the ground, but..." She shrugged. "Silly little bitch. She was just like you. Careless."

And she continued to blather on and on. Most of what she said made no sense. She talked about the cruelty of the doctors she visited, the incompetence of the counselors she'd spoken to, and the co-workers who judged her. It was a never-ending list of people who she thought had done her wrong.

Finally, we were out of the city, and she seemed to relax a little and slow down. I braced myself, looked into the side mirror: nothing, no cars, no lights. The road in front and back was shrouded in darkness. I readied myself. If she slowed down below forty, I planned to throw myself out of the car. I looked out through the side window. Everything was a blur and almost pitch black. And then I lost my nerve. I figured I'd probably break my legs, or worse, my head, and then I'd really be done for.

I had no choice but to wait.

"So," she said. "I bet you're wondering what I did with all the money I took from those guys." She smiled proudly. "All together over the years I've collected almost five thousand dollars."

"Five thousand?" I asked. "How the hell many have you killed?"

"Your cop friend was number eleven. D'you know that tight piece of shit had only fourteen dollars in his wallet? Geez, I heard cops didn't get paid much but fourteen dollars..."

My guts almost turned inside out at her words.

"I'm sure you used it to feed your habit. Steroids, right?" Her smile faded. "Screw you," she snarled.

"I saw your little kit in your apartment. In the bathroom."

"You were in my home?"

"We sure were... So what's with all those pictures on the walls and in the bathroom? And what about the hormones you bragged you were taking? I didn't find them. How long have you been a junkie, Natalie?" I asked, looking out of the side window, trying to gauge if the car was slowing.

I turned and looked at her. *Is that a tear?*

"You had no right to do that," she whispered. "How would you like having strangers go through *your* things?"

She'd lowered her hand. It was resting on the center console, the gun still pointing at me, her finger still on the trigger.

"You're wrong there. I had every right. I had a search warrant. You've got a lot of baggage going on in there. Come on, Natalie. Give it up. You can't win. I'm a senior police officer. You kidnapped me. They'll be on you like a duck on a June bug."

"They won't find me. I'll just disappear. I almost have enough for the down payment. I'll be a new person, a perfect person. I'll get a job, a good job, a man's job."

"In your dreams," I said. And then I saw lights in the side mirror, a car was approaching from the rear and it was approaching fast.

"I've never killed a woman," she said. "Not ever. I was brought up never to hit or hurt a woman, but I'm looking forward to killing you. I'm gonna shoot you dead, then I'm gonna shoot you in the back of the head..." she tailed off, dreamily. She was losing it.

Then she started to slow the car down. I watched the

speedometer, then the headlights behind us, then the gun in her hand.

"It's really fun, you know, to shoot someone in the head. And it's even funner shooting them in the back of the head, from the back seat."

Funner? What the hell kind of word is that? I thought, as I prepared myself to pull the door handle and roll out.

"See, I get to watch when I do it from the back seat. When I'm still steering the car, and I pull the trigger like this," she said as she raised the gun and pointed it again at the side of my head, "I don't get to see what happens... not really."

I squeezed my eyes shut and clenched my teeth. But Natalie just started laughing and lowered the gun again, her wrist on the center consol.

"See, when I sit in the back seat and put the muzzle to the back of the head and pull the trigger... You can actually see the head expand as the gasses fill it, then the slug. You know, you can't hardly hear it. It's like the head is a silencer... weird." She was all dreamy again. It was like she was a completely different person, and I wondered if maybe it was Natalie, not Nate. Then her voice suddenly changed, hardened and she snarled, "I can't freakin' wait to see your tiny brains splattered all over the windshield."

That would be Nate, I thought, my hand now on the door handle. *Come on, bitch. Slow down. Just a little more.*

"You're not going to get away with it, Natalie. Killing one cop has put you on the Chattanooga Most Wanted List. Killing me will make you public enemy number one. You won't even get out of town."

"I am not Natalie!" she screamed. She began beating

the steering wheel with her left hand. She spewed out a string of obscenities, naming me, the department, and anyone else she could think of. She'd lost it; she was spluttering. It was almost as if she was speaking in tongues except the words weren't Divinely inspired, but a raging diatribe of filth and hate.

"I'll teach you," she screamed. "You'll learn!"

And she slammed on the brakes. I wasn't prepared for it. I'd chosen not to fasten my seatbelt in the hope I might be able to jump out of the car. My head hit the dashboard. I saw stars. Everything went white. For several seconds I could see nothing. I sat up, blinked, put my hand to my head. Nothing helped. My brain was reeling; it wouldn't function.

"Bitch!" I heard her snarl. "Bitch, bitch, bitch... Frickin'... frickin' bitch. I'll frickin' teach her to screw with me. Nobody frickin' screws with me, not no hoity-toity bitch, that's for frickin' sure."

I heard the driver's side door open. I shook my head, trying desperately to clear it, but before I could, my door was flung open and Natalie had her gun in my face.

"Get out of the car, bitch," she hissed.

I shook my head, raised my hand to push the gun away from my face, then screamed in pain as she brought it down hard across my thumb. I tried to turn my head to look at her, and it was then I knew I was in trouble. I could barely see at all, and what I could see was fuzzy, out of focus, blurred. And I couldn't think, couldn't focus my thoughts, and I was sure there was something wrong with my hearing, too, because when Natalie screamed at me, it sounded like she was inside a giant clamshell.

"I'm going to enjoy this. You just wouldn't learn. You just..."

She grabbed my arm and pulled. I fell sideways out of the car onto the grass shoulder. I struggled to my knees. She kicked me in the ribs.

"I told you, didn't I?" she yelled. "I told you. I said I'd teach you." She laughed, bouncing on her toes like a damned boxer. "Now. Tell me. What's my name?"

"Natalie Cassidy," I replied defiantly and received a kick to my shoulder that spun me over backward; my face slammed into the hard dirt beneath the grass.

"Come on," she said, punching the air with her fist, waving the gun in the other, and dancing on her toes.

"Say it again, bitch. I dare you! You... frickin'," and she screamed more obscenities and stamped on my fingers, and kicked my legs, and then my thighs as I tried to protect my head and ribs.

And then I saw the lights of the car. *Oh, thank God!*

I needed to do something. I couldn't risk her taking off running across the field. And then I saw another kick coming. I grabbed her foot, wrapped my arms around her ankle and tried to pull her down.

"Leggo!" she yelled and punched me in the back of the head.

I balled up and wrapped my body around her leg and held on tight, my eyes clamped shut. She continued to swipe at me with her fist, but her blows were awkward and carried no real weight.

The car lights disappeared.

"Ugh," I grunted, hanging onto her like a boa constrictor. It was all I could do, and I was embarrassed when I thought about it later: big bad old me hanging onto that pathetic little thing, but what the hell was I supposed to do? I couldn't see worth a damn, and I was hurting like I'd been put through a trash compactor.

Where the hell did that car go? I thought desperately. Was there a road back there? Did they see what was happening and turn their heads away and drive on by? I didn't know. I just kept right on hanging onto her leg. I knew she couldn't kick me. If she raised her free foot off the ground, she'd fall over.

I knew I had to do something more, and quick. The only thing that came to mind was something I'd learned at the academy during self-defense training: go for the genitals.

Okay, so Natalie wanted to be a man, she had better get prepared to be treated as such. I turned her loose and with everything I had, steeling my stomach, I brought both fists up between her legs. The double blow landed perfectly, but it didn't faze her one bit: the bitch was wearing some sort of padded cup, to enhance her manly appeal no doubt. She barely felt a thing and, if anything, she became even more enraged. I got to my knees, raised my hands and looked right into the barrel of her Glock 17.

"Goodbye, bitch." She smiled and placed the barrel of the gun against my forehead, her finger already white against the trigger.

30

_____

I don't remember exactly what happened next. From off to the side, out of the corner of my eyes, I caught a glimpse of a shadowy form come flying in from the cornfield. At first, I thought it was a deer, but then it slammed into Natalie, sending her spinning sideways. She somehow managed to twist in the air and land on her back with a thud. She grunted as she hit the hard ground. The gun discharged harmlessly into the air and flew out of her hand to land several yards away in a shallow ditch just beyond the hard shoulder.

Still on my knees, my hands on the ground in front of me, supporting me, my ears ringing from the noise of the shot, I looked to my left and saw the "cute little redhead" Natalie had thought she'd put out of commission straddling the woman, sitting on her belly, pounding the living crap out of her. Janet was not holding back. Her fists were hammering Natalie's face and I could hear her, Janet, sobbing loudly as she gave way to the feelings we all had for the woman who'd killed our friend.

And then another dark figure appeared, gun in hand. The other hand grabbed Janet by the collar of her jacket and hauled her off the now barely conscious Natalie Cassidy.

"Get your hands where I can see 'em, *now!*" Hawk yelled at Natalie. "I said, put your hands up. If you don't get your hands up..."

Janet stepped back and away, shaking her hands from the pain of her busted knuckles. Now I wasn't the only one with a busted lip; Natalie had one too.

Janet spit on the ground next to Natalie and with two long strides she was at my side.

"Don't move, Cap. Help is on the way."

"I'm okay," I said. Ha, no. I tried to say it, but my lips wouldn't move. The words came out as an incoherent mumble even I didn't understand. I ran my tongue over my lips. They felt like a couple of Polish sausages. I touched the bottom lip tenderly with my finger, not the split, and a small speck of blood came away with it. At some point, I must have bitten it. When that had happened I wasn't sure, but as the past several minutes came slowly back into focus, I figured it must have been when my face hit the dashboard.

"Just stay still, Kate," Janet said soothingly. "There's an ambulance on the way."

I looked up at her and couldn't help but think how far she'd come over the past two years, since the first case we'd worked together. She'd almost become the latest victim in a string of murders. She'd just saved my life, and now she was taking charge. She was a rookie no longer.

Hawk holstered his weapon and turned Cassidy over onto her stomach, wrenched her hands behind her back and cuffed her. She struggled like a demented cat, screaming about her rights. Hawk recited them to her, then stepped away, put his hands on his knees and scowled at her.

"If I thought for one minute," he snarled, "that I could get away with it, I'd pound your face into the dirt." Then he stepped forward again and yanked her up onto her feet by her cuffed wrists.

She was a mess, and I had no doubt that there would be an investigation into why she was as bruised about the face as she was. I didn't care. It was what it was; no regrets. It was one of those bridges we'd have to cross when we came to it. Why should I care anyway, about what had happened to her? She was a cold-blooded murderer, of five that I had personal knowledge of, and six more, according to her. I was to have been number twelve. *Lucky me!*

"How did you know where I was, Janet?" I asked as I tried carefully to stretch my lips.

"It was just dumb luck. Hawk and I were on Brainerd Road. He'd just had a phone call from forensics. The DNA from the Band-Aid in Jack Logan's car matched what the Marines had on file for Natalie Cassidy. That puts her in Jack Logan's car. He was excited.

"As I said, we were passing your place and he didn't want to wait until morning to tell you the good news, so we decided to stop by, maybe drink a glass of red to celebrate. We'd just pulled through the gate into your complex when we saw Cassidy walking you toward your car. Hawk wanted to rush her right then, but I knew she had a gun and I was afraid she'd shoot you before we could stop her. So we decided to follow you.

"Even when she pulled over, we weren't sure what to

do. So we drove on by. Hawk turned off the lights and pulled over, and I jumped out and ran through the cornf— geez, Kate, that was really scary, in the dark, and all. Anyway, by the time I reached you, you both were out of the car and I could see... Well, that's when I lost it."

"Wow," I mumbled. "Thank God you did. She was just about to pull the trigger."

"They're coming," Janet said. "I can hear the sirens."

I could hear them too.

"There's something else," Janet said.

"Janet, I don't know if I can handle any more. Okay, go on. What is it?" I rubbed my forehead. My face was swollen. It felt like my skull was trying to push out through my skin.

It was right about then that two ambulances arrived. The paramedics helped me walk to the nearest one, and I sat down on the tailgate to listen to what Janet had to say.

"Tilly Montgomery came in earlier," she said. "She's still there locked up in an interview room. She talked to Ann for almost a half-hour. When they were done, Ann took her to Room B and locked her in and left her there, so she could come and talk to me. Apparently, something had spooked Tilly. She told Ann that she had a prior conviction for lewd behavior toward a minor, a five-year-old boy. She was concerned because she knew what happened to child molesters in jail."

"So what?" I asked. "Why would she go to jail for a prior?"

"Not for the prior," Janet said, shaking her head. "For molesting and aiding and abetting Cassidy."

"What?"

"Yep, apparently she's known for years what Cassidy's been up to. She even feared for her own safety, so she kept it to herself. She said if Cassidy confessed, it would all come out and she'd be screwed, so she wants immunity. In return, she said she'd testify against Natalie. She said Cassidy is responsible for nine murders that she knows of, and there may be more. I guess it's your lucky day, Kate; you get to clear up your cold cases," Janet said. "Maybe you should buy a lottery ticket."

I tried to laugh, but I couldn't; it hurt too much. So I huffed and tried to smile. What the hell I must have looked like, God only knows.

"Oh yeah," I said wryly. "I look like I got lucky, don't I?"

We sat together and watched as they escorted Natalie to the second ambulance. Just as they were about to pass by, however, she made them stop, and she smiled at me.

"You think you've won, don't you?" she said. "Well you haven't. I'll get my surgery in prison, you know, and I won't have to pay for a thing."

One of the paramedics tried to hustle her on past, but she looked back, and she scowled. "And then, missy, I'll be back to pay you a visit." She made an obscene gesture with her tongue and laughed... No, she cackled, like the damn witch that she was, and the EMTs hauled her away by both arms, and up into the back of the ambulance and slammed the doors.

I wouldn't see her again for almost two weeks. I didn't even get to do the interviews; Janet had that pleasure.

"Okay," one of the other EMTs said to me, "let's get you loaded. Up inside, please, and onto the gurney with you."

"I don't need that," I said.

"Why don't you just relax, Detective? Let us make that call. You've been through a tough time." It wasn't really a question, and they didn't give me a choice. In fact, they paid no attention to my protests at all.

Once they had me loaded, they began to question me. No, I'm not seeing double. You're holding up three fingers. Yes, my lip hurts. Yes, I have a headache. No, I'm not dizzy, well, not much, and on and on it went until finally they shut the doors, turned on the siren and away we went to Erlanger Hospital.

It seems funny now, but I remember the ride out at gunpoint seemed to last for hours, though it couldn't have been much more than twenty minutes or so. The ride back to the hospital seemed to be over almost before it had begun. Before I knew it, I was being unloaded into the emergency room. And then time really did stand still. They were busy that night, really busy, and I guess that since I wasn't bleeding out through my eyeballs, I was the low man on the emergency room totem pole; I didn't see a doctor for almost an hour.

My head still hurt, and that bothered me a lot. I was beginning to think that maybe I did have a concussion after all, but not from what had happened that night. I'd been having problems ever since Natalie had jumped me outside The Sovereign.

And then I got to thinking again. Yep, I know. I'm my own worst enemy when it comes right down to it, and I couldn't help but think how different things would have been if I'd only followed orders, done what I was supposed to and gone to the doctor. If I had, Miller would still have been alive... and maybe, just maybe, this whole nasty business could have been—

"Ah, there you are," a familiar voice said, interrupting my thoughts. I turned my head and saw the smiling face that went with the voice.

"I heard they had brought you in. I was waiting for you, but you didn't turn up. I was wondering what had happened to you. Now I know. How are you feeling, Captain?"

I chuckled as Doctor Joon Napai stepped into my little space.

"I was on my way to see you, Doctor. Honest Abe, I was," I said. "But I got... sidetracked."

"Yes. So I was told," she said, as she took a pen flashlight from her breast pocket and stepped to the side of the bed. "Look up, please. Hmm, now down... and the other... hmm."

"Will I live, Doc?"

"Undoubtedly, Captain. What happened to you? A cage fight perhaps? A bar brawl?" She pointed at my lips with her penlight.

"You should see the other guy," I said and tried to smile.

"Yes, so I heard. Well, you will not be leaving here tonight. I will order an MRI for first thing tomorrow morning."

"Thank you," I said. "I should have told you before. I've been having some real headaches, and dizzy spells. Nothing seemed to help. Sleep, eating or not eating. Aspirin. Wine." I shrugged.

"Well, we shall see," she said. "In the meantime, I suggest you try to get some rest. I'll have the nurse bring you an Ambien." She smiled kindly... and I started to cry.

She sat down beside the bed, picked up my hand and said, "It will be all right you know. You're just having a reaction. There's nothing to worry about."

"I know," I said, "and it's not that I'm worried. It's just..." And then I shut down.

She nodded sympathetically and said, "It is not your fault, any of it, not what happened to your young redheaded partner, Janet, or the officer that was killed in the line of duty."

"Miller? How do you know about that?" I asked.

"Word gets around. Doc Sheddon called me. He was worried about you. He said I should keep an eye on you. He attended to... Miller, you say his name was?" I nodded. "He attended to his remains."

I wiped my eyes, careful not to bump my sore lip. I looked at her. She was so calm, so... together. I wanted to say something, but there was nothing to say. For the first time since the Jack Logan case was handed to me, I was at a loss. It was over, done with, finished. No more insane deadlines, no bodies piling up, no one breathing down my neck, not even the Chief. The case was closed, wrapped up in a nice neat little bow, but you know what? I still felt like crap, and I told her so. All she did was click her tongue and shake her head.

"It's all about the anticlimax, you know, and your sense of loss, of course."

"His funeral is in two days," I said. "I'll never be able to keep it together, Doctor. I'll be a mess."

"And that is okay. You can be a mess. No one will blame you for that, and you will not be the only one."

I was released the following afternoon with strict instructions to go home and stay there for the next week; the only exception being that I could attend Miller's funeral.

The MRI had revealed nothing but a slight swelling of the brain and...

"How are you feeling today?" Doctor Napai had asked when she visited me earlier that morning.

"Fine, I think."

"Good. Well, you will be pleased to know that you do not have a concussion. Your head must be hard as a rock."

"I remember my father saying something similar when I was growing up."

She chuckled and said, "I am sure that he did." She stuck her hands in her coat pockets and smiled down at me.

"So what about the headaches?" I asked. "The loss of appetite, the pain at the back of my eyes? What's all that about?"

"Stress, Detective. Nothing more than stress. Something you will have to learn to live with... By the way, when did these symptoms begin? Can you remember?"

I thought about that for a minute, then I realized what she was getting at, and I nodded. They began when Harry Starke left the police department and I had to go it alone, but I didn't tell her that. I felt better just knowing.

"Years ago, when I received my first case as lead detective," I said. "And they've stayed with me over the years, but more so since I received my promotion to Captain..."

She nodded again. "As I thought. New responsibility. Stress. As far as your skull and brain are concerned, there is a little swelling, but that will get better quite quickly. Other than that, your head looks normal."

"So, when can I go home?"

"This afternoon, if you promise to be good. Detective, I am going to prescribe something for you and I want you to take some time off—"

"What for?" I asked, interrupting her. "If I don't have a concussion then—"

"Detective, you may not have a concussion, but you *are* suffering from Post-Traumatic Stress Disorder."

PTSD? I was stunned.

"Now, I know there are many doctors who prescribe drugs to treat the disorder," she continued. "I do not. I'm going to prescribe a very mild sleeping pill, and I am going to recommend that you talk to someone. That is it."

"A shrink? I don't think so. Look, I know what you're thinking. I know I broke down yesterday, but that was just a reaction. You said so yourself. I don't need a shrink. That lunatic who shot Miller, she needs a shrink. I don't need to talk to anyone. Especially not some kid fresh out of college who couldn't even imagine some of the stuff I've seen, let alone what happened to Lennie. No. I won't do it." I stared back at her.

"Oh, I think you will, Captain. I will not allow you to go back to work until you have completed twenty hours of therapy with a psychologist." And she looked at me as if to say *checkmate*.

"Damn it, Doctor... Okay, you win. Now, can I get out of here, please?"

And so that's what happened. She released me, I called for an Uber, and I went home and, for the most part, I did as I'd been told. Sheesh, I had to. I hadn't but stepped into my apartment that afternoon when Chief Johnston called and told me he'd have me shot if I even tried to step foot inside the police department until my seven-day respite was up.

As I expected, Hawk and Robar visited me a couple of times, but as far as work was concerned, they clammed up; I couldn't get a word out of either of them, not gossip, not anything. It was their idea of tough love. But that wasn't the worst of it; even Janet was holding out on me.

"Can't do it," she said when I called in to get the status on a couple of things I'd had on my mind. "It's doctor's orders, Cap. You are off for the week. If I break the rules and the Chief finds out, he'll have me back filing reports, and that ain't gonna happen. Be a good captain and do as you're told for once."

"You cheeky little... Just you wait till I—"

"Bye, Cap," she said, and hung up, leaving me staring at the blank screen of my iPhone. *Damn it!*

I did get to go to Miller's funeral the next day after Doctor Joon released me. It seemed to me that every off-duty cop in the Chattanooga tri-state area was also there.

Me? I accompanied his mother, who did more to help me than any doctor ever could. I held her arm throughout the service, trying to hold it together for her. But you know, when it was over that sweet lady took me aside, took both my hands in hers, and said, "You mustn't do it, you know, blame yourself. He wouldn't want that." She had tears in her eyes.

"He talked about you... a lot," she continued. "He thought so much of you." She patted my hand.

I looked down into her soft blue eyes and felt my own eyes begin to water.

"Lennie wanted to be a policeman all his life, ever since he was a little boy," she said. "He never wanted to be anything else..."

She paused for a moment, squeezed my hands and

continued, "When he was just a little guy, fourteen or fifteen years old, I remember asking him, 'But honey, what would I do if you got hurt?' He said, 'Mama, if I died in my uniform, I'd be happy knowing I'd helped make the world a better place.' It's the God's honest truth. He did, he said those words to me."

I looked down at her, and I lost it. I burst into tears. I cried and I cried, in front of everyone. I put my arms around her, and we just stood there, holding each other. I tried to tell her how sorry I was, and that I wished I'd done so many things differently. But she would hear none of it.

And so, almost three weeks later, I stood in front of the mirror looking at my reflection, recalling that awful day when we laid Lennie Miller to rest. The display of respect had been amazing. You see it on TV: hundreds of officers, motorcycles, and it's impressive, but to see it in your own hometown, for one of your own, for one of your friends... Almost eleven hundred officers, the mayor, the sheriff, Chief Johnston, Harry and his entire staff including my old friend TJ Bron. It was beautiful, but it was something I never want to go through again.

After the funeral we, that is me, Hawk, Robar and Janet, we went to the Boathouse for lunch, not that I felt like eating... none of us did. I remember it was a cold, clear day with not a cloud in the sky. We sat together inside by one of the windows. The river was quiet that day, a ribbon of dark glass that meandered almost imperceptibly slowly toward the city center. It too seemed to recognize the solemnity of the occasion.

We talked shop for a while, but not about the Cassidy case. When I think about it now, the conversation at the table that day was forced. I think now that each of us would rather have been anywhere else but staring out of the Boathouse window that day. But we were there to pay our respects to Lennie, and that's what we did. We raised our glasses to his memory and in celebration of his short life, drank a couple of beers, and told stories about him through the tears.

Me? No matter what they said, no matter what anyone said, I still couldn't shake the feeling that I was to blame; still can't. Oh, they all tried to console me. It was the nature of the game, they said; we lay our lives on the line every day, they said; you never know when it's your turn, but we do it anyway... blah, blah, blah. They all meant well, I knew that. They were such a great team. But with Lennie gone, there was a hole in the dynamic.

I remember we tossed back quite a few drinks that day, but they had little to no effect. When we left the Boathouse, we didn't go back to work; we all went home.

Cassidy is still awaiting sentencing. I was right, she did get a hotshot lawyer. Some TV personality type from Atlanta more interested in himself than his client. Sure, he made a big deal of the transgender thing, and the way his client had been treated, even demanded retribution for the beating she'd taken. But it went nowhere. When he saw what she'd done to me, and Hawk had testified that Cassidy had received her bruises while violently resisting arrest, he dropped it. He did manage to cut her a deal, though. The ADA, Larry Spruce, agreed to take the death penalty off the table if, in return, she'd plead guilty. She did. She confessed to a total of eleven murders and revealed where the bodies were hidden.

Me? I completed my twenty hours with the psychologist, a young PhD by the name of Holly Ferris. Did she do me any good? I think so. She must have thought so too, because I was released as fit to return to work yesterday, Friday. My first day back in the office would be on Monday and I was looking forward to it, sort of, but we won't get into that now.

So, there I was, staring at myself in the mirror, early on a Saturday evening, three weeks after Lennie Miller had been laid to rest. I was wearing a black skirt and a white blouse with a light blue blazer. I thought I looked nice, but professional. Not too fancy, but respectful and modest.

When my doorbell rang, I almost jumped out of my skin. I went to the intercom, pressed the button, and said I'd be right down. I checked myself in the mirror one more time, grabbed my purse and keys and headed downstairs. I was nervous. I'd never done anything like this before, but I was sure that Chief Johnston and Doctor Ferris would approve.

I opened the door and... my heart flipped. He was freakin' gorgeous. The man stood at least six-four. He was wearing a dark blue suit with a stiff, white button-down shirt and red tie.

Oh m'God. Are you serious?

"Sergeant Dorman?" I asked. It was all I could do to get the words out without stuttering.

He nodded. "Detective Gazzara?" It was that same deep soothing voice I'd heard over the phone.

"Yes, but please, call me Kate."

The End

Thank you. I hope you enjoyed reading *Cassidy* Book 7 in the Lt. Kate Gazzara series as much as I did writing it. If you did, and you'd like to read the next book in the series, *Georgina*, just CLICK HERE or simply copy and paste this link. https://readerlinks.com/l/1079919

Again, thank you,

Blair Howard

ACKNOWLEDGMENTS

As always, I owe a great deal of thanks to my editor, Diane, for her insight and expertise. Thank you, Diane.

Thanks also to my beta readers whose last-minute inspection picked up those small but, to the reader, annoying typos. I love you guys. Thank you.

Once again, I have to thank all of my friends in law enforcement for their help and expertise: Ron, Gene, David for firearms, on the range and off. Gene for his expertise in close combat, Laura for CSI, and finally Dr. King, Hamilton County's ex-chief medical examiner, without whom there would be no Doc Sheddon.

To my wife, Jo, who suffers a lonely life while I'm writing these books: thank you for your love and patience.

Finally, a great big thank you goes to my oh so loyal fans. Without you there would be no Kate, no Harry, Tim, Doc... well, you get the idea.

FREE BOOK

Now for a little something extra. You've just read Book 7 in the Det. Kate Gazzara series so you're up to date, at least for now, but be on the lookout for Book 8, Elizabeth, due out on May 31, 2020.

My question is, then: would you like to try something new, for free? How about I send you Harry Starke Genesis... for free? If you're a fan of Stuart Woods, Baldacci, Connelly, Coben and Hoag, you should get to know Harry Starke. He's a detective, dedicated, dark, dangerous, driven, and has a wicked sense of humor. He's addictive: you can't read just one. Click here to download your free copy of Genesis